Rebecca is a 44yr old woman who is blessed to have the people she does in her life.

Some say she is strong willed with a mysterious side and independent as well as nurturing.

She loves her family and appreciates those whom have supported her along the way of this journey called life, which is leading her to her great destination.

She is me, I am R.A. Bullis.

THE ANGEL
INSIDE HER,
AND THE
FOUR KINGS.

UNEDITED VERSION

R.A. BULLIS

authorHOUSE®

AuthorHouse™
1663 Liberty Drive
Bloomington, IN 47403
www.authorhouse.com
Phone: 833-262-8899

Published by AuthorHouse 05/26/2021

ISBN: 978-1-7283-5729-4 (sc)
ISBN: 978-1-6655-2239-7 (e)

CHAPTER 1

Legend has it that long ago an angel of grace and love would fall to the ground and emerge again inside a small child. A female child that was born in the Autumn month of October.

It would happen when the green leaves start to change colors to orange, red, yellow, and even brown. Then they would gracefully fall to the ground.

There was something to this legend about the angel that fell with grace, who would enter this said female child.

This female child would not grow up as the other children, for her home was not warm and loving. It was said that she would grow up in a lonely, corrupt, and an abandoned family.

A place where everyone was just out for themselves. They never had time for affection or compassion. This would be something she would always try to teach herself.

She would start to learn about weird things that would happen within her and markings that would start to appear on her body.

She had to be masked. If humans knew of HER being an angel, they would seek her out and put her on display for all to see.

Legend also says that the little girl would grow up and not even know her own name because she was never given one. When the time was right and there was compassion, she then would receive her name.

But throughout her journey she would be given a temporary name.

So in 1976 the little girl was born to an army man and an aspiring nurse in the Autumn. But this Autumn was like no other, it was the worst snow storm in history. She would be stuck in the house for a long time.

She would figure out things to do and try to figure out what these things on her back were for. She would hide what looked like burn marks.

Chapter 2

In the next few weeks, it would be her ninth birthday.

As days came and nights went by, she would grow into a beautiful, little girl. It was time, her birthday was right around the corner. This would be just no ordinary birthday.

For on her ninth birthday something would happen to her when she laid down for bed that night.

She started seeing visions of what she did not know. She felt funny as her whole body would tingle, and this would be the start of her unbeknownst powers, or let's just say gifts.

This would make her very afraid to go to sleep at night. She would try to reach out to her mother because she was not understanding what was happening to her.

She would try to explain to her mother the visions she would see on her wall at night, and the tingling feeling she started having. This made her afraid to sleep at night, as if she were frozen in fear.

Some of the things she would see looked like a goat faced man with horns. Later she would find out what all this meant, but it was not the only thing that was going on.

The tingling feeling was her senses trying to tell her something she needed to know about. This was her intuition calling to her.

When this happened the hair on her arms would stand up. She would have cold chills and then get very warm. This happened when she would start to fall asleep, she would see visions.

Always trying to understand this, she would so try to get her mother to help her.

Her mother would always push her aside, she felt she never had time for her child. She was too busy trying to focus on what she felt would get her a better career so she could make a better life for her children.

She would always tell HER she had a wild imagination and to go back to sleep before she woke the other children. HER mother would always tell HER if she did not stop she'd be grounded. HER mother never stopped to listen to HER.

Chapter 3

Her brother E would always try to comfort HER for they were close. HER's sister was there too, but not as much as her other sibling.

She used to tell her siblings about stories she would make up, or how she'd love to see the world and travel.

Travel to somewhere other than where she was at, where she lived, and the life she had. However, she loved her family. She made a pact and vowed to always protect her loved ones, and anyone that was close to her.

For they would know HER.

So she would go back to bed and lay awake and wonder what it would be like to go out and explore the world. She lived a very sheltered home life.

She would dream of the travels, and of other lands, and the nature and beauty in them. What would it be like just to stay—even for a moment—and breathe in something new.

As time went on and her birthday was upon her, legend had it that on the ninth day of the ninety-ninth year she would get her first gift.

The main gift bestowed upon HER was empathy. And as time went on she would start to receive other gifts on certain days, times, and years as the moments of her life went on.

The gifts she would receive were: First, on her ninth birthday she would receive empathy.

On her sixteenth to twentieth birthdays she would experience weird energetic flows. These flows of energy would come and go, along with her visions. She would start to have predictions, but only when she slept or drifted off in a daze. This it did not happen all the time. Not yet, anyway. But when time passed, she would eventually get those gifts in full force.

CHAPTER 4

The next gift would be on her twenty-second birthday. It was the gift of precognition.

Then, on her twenty–seventh birthday, it was psychokinesis. She would learn to use her mind to move things. It started only when she was under pressure, but she would learn how to control things on a normal basis as she grew older.

Her thirty-six birthday would be telepathic gifts. She could start to hear people talking and could hear their thoughts. She was able to talk to people through her mind.

She could read people just by being around them. Shaking their hands, or just by their touch, she could see into the future. Just by touching their hands or hugging them, she would see flashes of something that was going to happen for them or against them.

Her forty–fifth birthday, well let's just say this would be her marriage date. At this point everything was falling into place. It started when she was forty–three, her gifts were in full bloom. These gifts would be with her for the rest of her life as she'd gratefully take them with HER.

From birth, she received from God and the universe, the gifts of clairvoyance, shapeshifting, psychometry, cytokinesis, and invisibility. She knew nothing about all this and they scared her. She always refused to believe. Until her forty-third year that she was alive, she would learn to accept all the gifts she possessed. Once she understood them that is, and most of all accepted them.

These gifts, she would receive all at once and then emerge into what she was meant to be. Eventually, she came to accept these gifts.

She'd have to go through life with people calling her crazy, weird, and more, for people are cruel. She, however, would overcome this in time.

CHAPTER 5

She was beautiful inside as well as out however she would deal with the name calling by reading books, writing poetry, painting, and helping others. This would help her cope with how she was feeling. Most of all, it made her happy just to see a smile on someone else's face.

Since she was typically always on her own, she became a survivor. People found it hard to believe that she could be who she really was, genuine, loyal, and honest. She almost always stood up for what she believed in. However, she had to learn to stand up for herself and believe in what she had been preaching to others in her own town and people she came across.

(Even though to those who she felt weirdly odd against, she'd wear masks, till the one, that would come along and break then, For they would know the real HER.)

Those who did her wrong, caused her pain or harm, she'd forgive them. But she never forget those who left her side. For she would never have left theirs.

She would eventually leave them alone and move forward. For they were of no good will, and no good for her to be around.

This left her to where she would always try to remain independent. Whenever others would help she'd always try to show HER appreciation and help them in return.

If they helped her in any way, in return she would help them wholeheartedly. It was a form of repayment for their genuine kindness, and it always spoke to her heart.

She would shut down being in her head because her biggest fear was abandonment and not knowing stability. She would figure this out by her forty-fifth birthday. It's never too late to learn, and she would be okay with this, she'd tell herself.

However on this day something extraordinary would happen to and for HER. What would it be? HER curiosity started to get to her as she kept on her journeys.

She had a vision and felt she had to love herself first. She had to do what made HER happy instead of always trying to please others or control bad outcomes. So she'd let go and let God and the universe do their jobs.

She was finding her strength, and she was finding her real calling and her worth. To her this would be much more important than she could ever imagine.

And with this legend at the end of her journeys, something strange would happen with HER and on her paths, this you will surely find out what it will be.

CHAPTER 6

As HER ninth birthday was passing, they got terrible news of her father's passing, and so this caused HER mother to struggle alone with her three children, and try to do what she thought was best.

Well HER being the second child born was nine times out of ten forgotten about and so she would play outside to ease HER troubled mind or go to writing for this helped get this off her mind.

She would climb the trees, make forts, build bridges and play in the mud.

She would make up her own world, where it was safe and loving, she would let no one in, for no one ever could hold the key.

She made a wish one night under the starry sky, this wish she'd tell no one about for if she did, they had to be some kind of special.

With the loss of her father an mother always gone, off to find their own happiness.

She pushed herself to the limit and deep inside knew she had a pair of wings for there were markings placed upon her as a smaller child.

Always feeling she could fly, she just needed to learn how, but she would need a teacher. This special day she felt pain like no other in her back. The pain was between her shoulders blades, as she fell to the ground screaming, no one could hear her cries. This calming feeling came over her as she heard a voice say, everything is going to be okay.

Who would be this voice? what was this voice? As would pass before her journey would come to an end she would find out.

She picked herself up and she started to flap her wings, for that was where the pain came from, Her wings grew right out of her.

She found that the wings started flapping on their own. She had no control over them and so she flew. The girl soon gets to where she was able to tame them.

Well tried, she flew again a fell but little by little she watched her wings grow bigger and bigger, as so did she, flourishing.

She found herself waiting wondering and watching for what she did not know but would eventually find out. Time went on she would go back and forth about this new found secret.

She had to learn to get her wings to disappear as she would walk up to the house. Her mother, brother and sister could know nothing of this.

She would learn to tuck them in and when no one was around expand them out, and fly.

She would learn how to make her wings dissipate and hide inside of her back. One day retracting in they would not come back out, as if they were cut off. She would not understand this as she had got attached to them. She had so much fun and peace when she was flying. What was happening and why? She would cry out as if she lost apart of herself. She fell into a depression; it was a deep one.

Things as if they were not bad enough for her, started getting worse.

There would be the markings of where the wings once were, now she could not think of this. She had a lot going on, a lot to process. Her mother took off one day and never returned.

She was now alone, her sister left to stay with another family and her older brother went off on his own, he vowed though he'd always be around if ever needed.

Not being able to bare this thought of her whole family breaking up, she knew she had to leave as well, trying to reach out to others and she knew she couldn't tell them everything for she'd end up in foster care.

What was going on with her as she could not take it any longer and no one would listen to her. She decided maybe it was best she leave and do what she dreamed of.

So outside one day, she ventured off out back of her home where the woods were.

Where she was told never to go, however as her curiosity got the best of her she felt invited in.

She would go where the Lilly's bloomed and cattails stood by a glistening lake for she felt she would be fine and safe there.

She sat down to write for this is where she would find some kind of peace, the peace she found in her writings of poems and stories. She continued writing and writing and soon she would see a weird looking light sign ignoring this at first.

CHAPTER 7

She would soon see it again, a glimpse of a light. Wondering if it could be a lightening buggie thing, shaking it off she moved further an further into the woods, which unbeknown to her was an enchanted place.

She heard and noise after this light flying around, was she there by herself? She wondered. Where was this noise coming from, a strong buzzing sound that got louder and more annoying.

No, for you see it was an angel spirit but disguised as a fairy, shaking this off, she started moving further and further into the woods.

She came about face, and was staring at the light right in her face. Swishing her hands back and forth she looked again, it was gone. So as she continued to walked about five hundred steps ahead.

Seeing the light again, appearing right in front of her not moving but in a stillness, she then heard a voice speak out, Hello. I am Amorella, as she started to form into a fairy.

What are you? she asked. Poking the fairy, you're so tiny. Amorella replied in a firm voice, I am a fairy. What are you? You are so big, buzzing around her head. She said, I am a human.

What is your name? She asked the little girl, she replied I don't think I have one, and I do believe I am lost. For I've never been to these parts of the woods let alone here.

Never before have I ventured out away from home. I think I have gone too far away from my where house is.

Amorella said, I will guide you and show you around, come with me she said. The girl just smiled and said I have faith you can get me where I need to go. I need to find my home, I shall follow you. You must answer a couple questions for me though, Amorella said surely.

What would be your questions?

She asked how long would it take to get through the woods? Is the woods safe? She was worried about getting home to her siblings, her family.

Amorella replied, I don't know how long and the woods I have gone through have always been safe. I've heard of rumors about far off lands.

There are a lot of things in these woods, animals, creatures, mythical creatures as well, as far as humans, hmmm well you're the first one that I've seen. I heard there are others though, far, far off in a distance where we fairies do not travel.

We have been forbidden to go, the head fairy Venus wood never allow this, ever.

Amorella told her keep following me I'm going to take you somewhere and stop by my home first to let them know where I am going, she agreed.

Amorella was really taking her to see Venus and Bella for there was an ancient myth about a little human girl that would come along one day.

Then out of the blue, they knew there was something special about her and the gifts she would receive along her path.

As she followed Amorella through the woods they would come to a mysterious stump from an old ancient tree. Amorella would whisper a secret word, sherise and when she spoke this the dark brown spot on the stump, it had started opening as it inched open little by little, til the spot opened fully.

Inside was a amazing place they would walk inside and go through, she replied, I am to big, what shall I ever do? I need help don't leave me behind.

Hello, don't go Amorella, as she thought Amorella was gone. Amorella flew back to the opening of the tree.

Amorella said, silly me and laughing said sherise sherose and the girl shrunk just enough to fit inside the stump of the trees entrance way. Little by little slowly shrinking she told Amorella she felt funny, whow, whow she said. This feels weird and asked as she was shrinking when would she be able to go back to normal size, her normal size, not Amorellas size.

Amorella replied, when the spell wears off, it does not last long. I am new at this and I was told I should get my full magic soon. When we grow which isn't much she laughed and we pass out test we will get magic. We will be able to make spells and help others, the spells are only for our fairy dust nothing else.

We can shrink people, we can make them sleep, we can heal little wounds and we can make up some foods. It all depends upon what tests we graduate from. Our tests are harder than most and not all pass. We have to focus and try extremely hard.

This is just something we can do with some words and some little fairy dust for now.

The little girl would tell the fairy about how she was so mesmerized by the room she was walking in, for there were rubies and diamonds all around and the walls of the stump, Trimmed in gold.

As they walked through and Amorella flying all around her, speaking very fast.

She had told Her that there were others, do not be afraid for they are of good. They will not harm you, I must introduce you. Amorella said, you will like them oh I know you will. They are fun and loving, we have some fairies like Smiles that always plays jokes, he is the one friend,me and my friend always fly around these parts together.

Sometimes we get on our ants or butterflies to fly us when tired or at night we use our trusty fireflies that light up the night sky an guide us around .

She asked what others, who, what? Amorella explained there is other fairies. Like smiles and more mythical things in the woods like trolls, leprechauns and more for this we must hop to it, so we can get through these woods. As they kept walking they came to a red door off to the right of the tunnels.

What is behind that door Amorella? For I am starting to feel weird, tingles and cold and then hot. I think my intuition is growing. Amorella would explain, Through the red door was the room of rubies and there would be the fairy of all fairies, to be prepared. Well they went through the doors and there stood VENUS.

The goddess of all fairies and when Venus took one look at the little girl and in her eyes for a few minutes, it was in her eyes Venus knew she was the one to obtain a locket that was there waiting on her for many generations. During ancient times the ancestors brought this necklace to be protected from the evils that lurked all around them, as if they were in some kind of spiritual battle.

Venus agreed she would protect this special necklace until they returned or the true person it was meant for came along. The ancestors explained, that only one could obtain this and it would be a female child of the age nine. Venus had a feeling that this little one was the girl the ancestors spoke of.

Venus said, come with me something is waiting for you. The girl asked what is it Venus? She said it was in a secured case, there was a locket. Venus explained a little about the locket for she did not want to scare her with the horror of the opposite if it wasn't not the right female or person for that matter.

Venus continued to explain, little one it is a necklace make of rubies, diamonds and in the middle was a rare pearl, a pearl of love an success. The one it is meant for will surely find this.

The girl felt her heart beat fast she knew there was something about the necklace as they grew closer and closer to it. She was so drawn to it as if it was meant for her. Such a lavish necklace, one that she couldn't believe she could or would ever see in her life.

Something abruptly happened, a loud crash, bang, again a loud crash, bang. What was that the girl asked Amorella and Venus?. Venus told Amorella to keep her back for she didn't know if it was sworn enemies of the fairies.

A being of a pink glaring light, all of a sudden appeared before them. This was no enemy.

It was Bella a witch but of good, not of evil. The fairies tended to speak of in a very high respectful manner of her. Bella always would protect them and teach them spells to bring food for eating and ones for protection.

Only Amongst the fairies, Bella would teach the fairies and the little ones. The little girl had well heard about this witch but thought of her bad for she heard in her childhood stories from her mother.

She would be told to stay in bed or a witch would get her from her feet an take her if she got out of bed. Bella just said, that is not me, that would have to be my evil twin, Benikka. She was vanished a long time ago for doing such things and was stripped of her powers from the higher ups. Bella being made up of the love light would never do such a thing. You can trust her, the girl found it hard to but nevertheless tried. Venus would be sent to her as a truth. She would come to realize what her purpose truly is and what it has always been.

They would become stronger and would start to drive her mad, Bella would tell her for she knew the little girl was scared of these new found gifts .

Bella also explained, that there would be a lot of lessons for her to be able to get through. She could really understand all her new found gifts and ones she'd receive as time would pass.

First she had to learn a lot of lessons. Her ancestors wanted her to know everything she needed for her final out come, so they sent Bella. Bella would teach her somethings that she'd be able to use as far as spells and or manifestations that would help along her journey.

She would need to do somethings some would not understand. Bella was sent to HER, she felt as if she knew, whom her ancestors were or passed loved ones that sent Bella to her .

It had to be Jame a friend for life, only guy friend she would or could ever really open up to or would even really knew her for he always would see right through her or make her open up and her grandparents for that is all that really knew her, when they were alive.

Her loved ones for she thought of three and two that she would see out her bedroom if a blue light, ones that watched over HER as she grew.

Unbeknown to her they were, watching all around an from above. She would later find out whom these ancestors were and passed lived ones.

These ancestors had gathered around one day knowing she would find out her gifts and the ancestors knew that someday it would force herself to adventure out, away from her small secluded home in a tiny, city town.

Setting forth Bella told HER after along four months that she would have to go for she was being called back to the ancestry realm, she would have to go in a matter of minutes this made HER sad for Bella became like a mother to her for which she would never forget.

They hugged an Bella told HER forget me not for me an your ancestors are and will be watching over you.

When you look to the sky you will see us, shinning bright above an upon you dear child.

Take care, take care, take care, Bella said as she faded away she whispered, Amorella will take over and Venus will give you a message.

Pay close attention, and not another sound, she was tearing up but straightened up and with a brave face shook it off.

Looking towards Amorella and Venus, she acknowledged them and asked, what is next? Tell me, show me. I am ready to find out and I am willing to learn.I believe I've waited long enough. So with that Amorella and Venus started to guide her towards this place which would light up as she walked within the walls of the tunnels which now they were in the ruby room.

Soon Venus would explain, what was going on and what was about to happen. Amorella said, child be prepared for this is not to scare you. It will help you along your wondrou paths. Look forward, to what lies ahead for the end destination will be the greatest outcome you could you ever imagine. Treasure beyond your wildest dreams, remember it will be all you've ever wanted. Amorella and Venus brought forth the crystal case, you could see the necklace.

Venus would explain, that she thought the girl was meant for the necklace however there was an ancient spell placed upon it. If someone or something tried to take it, well for whomever tried to obtain and wear it something bad would happen to them.

It was meant, for only one and if it wasn't the person it was meant for, spells would be placed upon them an the spells would act according to their greed, or want, whatever the case may be.

The intent would be hundred times intensified. As in if they wanted it for greed that said greed would eat them up alive, and death of greed would be placed upon them.

Lots of these cursed items always ended up in not so good hands.

Ones it's not meant for if it was about power, they would live out their lives alone an in fear the power they possessed and freeze with the greatest of fears, that they had and would sur come to them. For it was about the power the necklace processed, it would power up and the person would combust with what their intentions were.

So you see the person had to be of pureness and had to have or be in good faith. Only then would the necklace call to them, they would be drawn to it. That would be whom the necklace would be for, the owner that the necklace had waited on for thousands of lifetimes.

Bella all of a sudden had appeared again, she said that the ancestors told her that she had to be there, when the person whom would find the necklace or they had to be taken to it, and if it was meant to be, that Bella herself had to confirm this, as so it was. Bella would take her along side Amorella to check out this beautiful locket an to see if in fact she would be the one it was meant for.

However, the one the locket was meant for would glow. The person the necklace was meant for would call out a word, not even they would understand and the necklace would know when this person had arrived.

So the girl whispered, and called out the words, as she said with an odd voice, rainbow warrior for she didn't even know what it meant but spoke it. Just then the crystal case light up bright glowing and opened for Bella said, I knew all along you were HER.

The necklace has responded, Bella told the girl to go grab the necklace. Take this, guard it closely for If in need I will personally protect you near or far. I will protect you from your enemies and those of not good intent.

Beware for there are these shadow hunters that are know to try to suck your life energy, right out of you.

Take this as a warning through your journey child. I am sorry to warn you this, for you see I am the guardian of the necklace. Thousands of years, I have guarded this precious piece, I am six thousand years old. Now you, my dear must protect it. I will not be far, when in need.

Many will come with swords, wands, cups an pentacles, and more. They will try to take this for it's of pureness and unconditional love so many longed for, an only a few will have in their lives but none have been able to obtain thus far.

This is my eagle of sight, it has an intuition of it's own and will fight to protect you, take him with you. He will be there to guide you when you most need him, for that is what he does.

Let my pet eagle now guide you along many paths, for you will find him useful. I must go now before I am found out by the others that wait and watch. You see, we are being watched by the others and only can say a few things to help you out or guide you to things. We can't say to much for they are watching from above.

There are things you must figure out on your own for you cannot mess with free will. My spell, being dressed as a commoner wears off soon. As Bella started off, she told HER I will be around near or far so don't freight.

All of a sudden, Saturn and Jupiter appear and told Amorella an HER the necklace is something earned, not given you must always remember this. When for on these journeys, it is best you keep it covered up and not lead on you have it.

NOW, you must be off for you have to start your journey and walk through the Forest of the Dark. Keep in mind that the shadow hunters often linger around these parts of the forests.

They will look for you, for you are the chosen one and you must fight through it, for they will try to steal your soul. The wind blowing all around, she was gone. On the journey they went, activating the winds, Amorella blew and hummed a whisper and it grew and grew, the winds.

Darkness all around them had started. Oh my GOD, would they get out of this? It was bad, crashing sounds all around them.

Things barely missing their heads, but when Amorella whispered her hums to the wind, she activated the wind Spirit and everything calmed down.

Before their eyes a Magician would appear, again before them and tell of these secret bridges they must cross but were hard to find.

He also would explain to HER that throughout her time he would appear before them on the paths, let's just say guidelines to follow. The Magician poofed out of sight so Bella had to explain.

Bella started explaining about how to over come these bridges and where to look for them.

Where about for they might be hard to find, she exclaimed. She also explained some dangers of the three bridges and what lies within or around them. She told HER, these bridges you will come across there will be three trolls, so beware, we must go now but as Venus and Bella told them, we will be near in time of need.

She had met other creatures in the tunnel caves like a chupacabra lamb, a zebness, a mana tail, and an elephantus. Which were all friendly and warmed up to HER really quick. She had played with them for days getting to know each an everyone of them. They made her smile an started warming the heart of this girl, whose heart a one time was gone.

The most important people to HER was Venus an Bella, she became close to them as they trained her and encouraged her to move forth.

We only could help you child for so long, now it time. you must set forth on your journey, time is wasting. Keep your head held up an held high, Venus and Bella told her. Everything will be okay, be gone and on your way. Amorella an her set off through the forest, they would come across two brothers Malkin, Marcell, and their sister Mierca they were the trolls that governed the bridges.

They soon passed they Crystalline Waterfalls in the middle of the woods where as they would come to the first of the few bridges. Amorella knew a troll would be there for it was Malkin the strongest, biggest, oldest troll. He jumped out to scare them, saying no one passes without paying a toll. The little girl spoke up an said, I have nothing to give to pass on your bridge but need desperately to pass. I have to so I can see the kings please, ohh please let us across. When I get to the king I will surely pay you and make sure you get whatever it is you are seeking.

Malkin said No, you must give me something now. How about the white purple flower and the light pastel purple one with gold flowers you hold in your hair. The ones she picked along her way, by the waterfalls that had slowly started to bring her out of this depression she was in since a small child. She did not want to part with them but knew she had to continue on her path, she would have to give them up. They were beautiful to look at and helped her mentally but the flowers were really of no use. Sadly the girl turned over the flowers for Amorella said, they can always come back an get more. She thought back on these rare flowers that she was drawn to for it was so dangerous to get them.

She was thinking about the flying squirrels that helped her when the rocks were falling all round them. How the squirrels had saved their lives and how the talking flying squirrels helped her with shelter and food.

She thought about how they had help her get the flowers, their names were Maliki an Manae. It was so dangerous as they had to go through the sphinxs the squirrels had grabbed them an up in the mountains. That way they would not be destroyed by the beams of red light that would beam out of the sphinxs eyes and fry them to oblivion.

Heck, she was thinking back about how this would happen when the sphinx's eyes would open. One sat on each side of this mountain and how a scary voice said, who is this that tries to pass?, for they will perish. The squirrels got HER passed the sphinxes, they no sooner crumbled an fell. When her an Amorella got to the mountain side, they bumped into the squirrels whom helped them with shelter and had hid them out. Because something of darkness on their trail, the squirrels had also helped them train for the sphinxs for as the legend of them terrified them just to speak of it for no one has ever passed the sphinxes. If someone dared tried them, they would be found dead and their ashes whisked away in the desert by the winds, and howling creatures. Come to find these howlers as they were called, were merely called wolves. So as the sphinxs were beaten at their own game. Amorella and the girl had survived because of Manae and Maliki.

CHAPTER 8

The squirrels took them back to their home, they fed Amorella and HER a feast of diffrent kinds of food. Amorella would give them a piece of the sphinxs head, pieces for they would be of great value. The other animals an creatures would come to them now, as the rulers of the mountain side.

They had stayed with the squirrels for about three weeks to gather their thoughts, and their strength for they would soon be on their way. It was not crystal clear, their path, for when the sphinxs fell and it made a barrier between the mountain tops, and to the ground crashing making it to where noone could cross.

The day after, the third week they had been with them they awoke to somethings from the squirrel like seeds, fire sticks, and a few pans that were very small but they could use them on their path, along with some lanterns for when darkened nights would come upon them. They said their good byes to the squirrels and were off to head to meet the king. They both at this point had to focus an let no one or thing distract them. The journey for HER was of great importance.

They did tell the squirrels they would see them again, but for now she was becoming hungry as well as Amorella and knew she must leave all that behind as well as her knew found friends, she had met. They stayed behind for that was their home. So off they went an came across a mulberry tree that was in full bloom, they couldn't believe it. Jackpot Amorella said, and they pulled out a nap sack off HER back and loaded up.

What could we make of these berries?, for we have to eat and it's been several days she said to Amorella. Amorella said, lets put it in this pan that the squirrels gave us and mash them up, let's find some thing we could use to mix with these berries.

They looked around and found some cactuses around this rockslide and dirt. Amorella told HER let's split this cactus open and mix with the mulberries and drink the fluid, hydration from juice of the cactus and eat the berries for nutrition.

There not being much of anything to eat or drink, they had to do what they must.

They would gather up as much fluid from the cactuses as they could find and put in a metal pan container to use to drink as they got thirsty. The food they would leave behind for it was to much to carry, so they would eat when or what they could, when they could find it.

As they ate and drank they headed walking South, soon they would run into someone but who would it be when they started fully on their path, for in the beginning they bumped into a Magician that had told then of these trees an said, each berries you eat is like eating a whole meal an will fill you up. However, there is a catch for each tree is guarded by a bunch of wild cats.

Watch out for especially the orange one. What about the orange one?, she asked. The Magician explained, he is magical an you have to fight off his tricky magic.You must block it, you must get through this to get to the first king here's a hint, you will blindly have to let faith alone guide you through.

HER being at this point was a bit nervous but nevertheless would shake it off and get out of her way and look ahead for she knew she had to move.

Listening to this Magician, he started to tell her things that would be coming for her along her path, full force ahead of them.

He would speak of the Ring of Luna and the sacred tattoo, and bits and pieces of other things as well.

Amorella wanting to know said, please we must know more. The Magician said, you can not know for now it will disrupt time and space, Amorella and you will find out when the time Is right.

Now I've said to much, this could go against me with the upper elder Magicians. They're the ones that protect all galaxies. There are many an they only send us to the special ones. The ones being of human or mythical, have the ability to look beyond this dimension, they are called the Secret Tower of the Order .

Go and set forth, REMEMBER WHAT I SAID. If the elders find out, they have the power to rewind time and make the day start all over again. Till they feel It's right, as of now they don't know I've told you anything. If this was to happen everything I told you will be as if I untold you what I have, goooo now.They appreciated the advice and the knowledge, knowing that bared great importance now, they had to get going.

Setting on their path they walked till they found a little area and set up for the night.

They looked an looked for a right spot to set up for the night. Amorella wanted to keep safe from evil doers, so she made HER look for a spot between four trees. That way they wouldn't be seen to the outside and become easy prey. At last, after finding shelter, they would soon be running into the cats and trying to plan for their up coming interactions with them.

Coming across the cats, Oh dear' look we've walked into on the path, watch out for the orange cat as they weaved and dodged the other cats throughout the path. There was the orange cat waiting for them to show their faces. Some of the cats would disappear and reappear, the girls fading in and out right before them. They could not be able to see the girls and had a advantage over the cats, this would make it hard for them to get out of this triangle tangle of a mess. The orange cat spoke and said, my, my, my, what do we have here?. Amorella said, we must pass, he said, not today you do not pass through. The orange cat said, some spell as he grew and grew to the size of a giant. He stopped and he said, you both will stay and be my prisoners for the times.

We've never had a human in our mists before let alone a fairy. So you see we can use her to barter for what we want and treasurers we seek.

Amorella said, no, no, no, sir, for this girl is special and is to see the four Kings in a timely manner. The longer we wait the longer it will take on our path for her to have a name.

Amorella flew around and around causing a little wind, telling her to run, as she did and got out the cats view an through the path, she prayed as she waited for Amorella .

She had waited for a few hours and at this point was worried, with tears in her eyes for at this point all she had was Amorella. She dropped to her knees and prayed again, she prayed about three more times and out of the blue. Finally, Amorella caught up with her and told her the orange cats magic tried to pull her back in the path as she was almost out. A few times this took place and she had to use all her little might I pull through with her fairy dust. Finally, getting to the trees where they were safe to set up camp. Amorella admitted to knowing a little more magic and could always make an illusion up, making things look as if they were never there, kind of like a hidden protection shield.

As she did this an they walked throughout the trees grabbing all the could the passed the orange cat as they had faith guide them. At this point they were so exhausted they finally began to set up camp at a little hut an snuggled up in an old hammock, that someone must of let behind on their travels and fell fast asleep.They awoke the morning dawn and after packed up not before Amorella wanted to make a breakfast. She found some fish in the near by lake and coconuts that had fallen from the trees, the mulberries let's not forget eggs from a magic spell she created. Amorellas magic at this point was growing stronger and stronger for if she sneezed whatever she was thinking would pop up, so she had to work on this, and the girls telekinesis. Her visions would become clearer as well and as for the girl, she too would gain magic in many different ways. To work on this, Amorella went into the woods while she slept but before breakfast, as she spent some time in the woods, she got hungrier and hungrier. She knew she had to get back to camp to make them something to eat.

Just as she was getting close she heard a eagle call to her, warning her what lays ahead and about the girls magic the eagle explained, as he started to speak to her told her he was sent by the higher ups the ancestors and that Amorella must know that the girl was born with magic in her heart and will be heighted with a stone.

This was the only way it could be unlocked is for HER to learn what she must or her magic could be gone forever, along with this, she must let down her wall around her heart.

As with her emotions even though done wrong many times before, and with that Amorella thanked the eagle an said, she would do all she could for HER.

Amorella was heading towards camp where she left HER to sleep and would let her know what the eagle told her as he flew away.

She started making a breakfast and she couldn't hold back any longer, an told her of the eagle an how it was sent by the uppers to warn them of certain things that the must pay attention too.

Well she wanted to know more, so Amorella told her and with that breakfast complete.

Amorella made a good breakfast out of the mulberries and with a little magic whipped up a delicious meal, after they picked up their bags an headed to a Field of Sunflowers.

They took a little time and played and laughed sitting in the middle of the meadows admiring the sensory. They packed up an headed on their way towards the second bridge, not before gathering up some sunflowers.

CHAPTER 9

They would later dry them out an use the seeds to eat, so they wouldn't go hungry.

As they approached the second troll, he jumped out an said, what do you have for me? I will not let you cross without. Marcellus said, I smell something good. Amorella and the girl said, we have mulberries, Marcellus said, I will take that an I'll take them all and so they handed them over, they walked, walked, and walked some more.

They knew Miera was the last troll they would have to face, the most scariest places of them all. So it was told, they would come to find out Mirea was way different, then originally they had heard about her. Little did they know Mirea was the kindest and gentlest one out of the three. For the first troll was rude, an the second one was a bully, she'd be the opposite of them. As night approached they came across the third and final bridge.

This shadow came closer an closer, Amorella looked at HER and said, this is frightening and all of a sudden Mirea jumped out and said, Nice to meet cha, tell me your names and I'll let you pass that's it and that's all.

Amorella said, her name and said, my friend doesn't have one that's why were on these journeys to find out her name. So Mirea said, I'll give her a temporary name her name will be Moonlight laughing they all rolled around in the grass an ground an just laughed and laughed.So dawn had approached and she allowed them to pass explaining they are headed to the valley of the clovers, she said thanks for all the laughs,for I've not laughed like that in years .

She said make sure y'all stop by sometime. We will surely have to do this again. We sure will try replied Amorella.

They came across a gazebo as they slept there an awoken to the morning sun and smell of fresh air they ate the rest of the mulberries she found in HER nap sack and drank from the spring that Amorella filtered through her magic. They could drink and off to the valley they went eating some sunflower seeds they had previously dried out at the gazebo.

Amorella whipped up a little magic for some real food like bacon and ham eggs and some coconut milk, she then would try to teach HER to use some of her magic that the eagle had told her about and with that she tried squinting her eyes an trying hard.

Amorella said think smarter not harder .let all the negative energies go. Let the positive energy flow in. Breath deeply in, hold it. Now breathe out slowly.

Take a deep breath let it come from down deep inside and let it out. Here try to move this coconut around an then crack it open. Finally after several tries she was able to move the coconut and seconds later would crack it in half, HER gifts were growing and growing and so was her intuition and telekinesis. So after breakfast the would head to the valley. Amorella would try to get her to focus on using these two gifts, for they were of importance.

Soon after trying for hours, she started to learn how to use and control these powers as they started getting stronger, Amorella said that it was enough training and they had to move forward to the valley.

She said to Amorella, I wonder what this valley has to hide? Know what I mean its like everything else had had a secret or something to over come, or some kind of a challenge.

I feel I want to give up with tears in her eyes. Amorella shouted nooo you hear me, you can do this.

You must do this, for all of us that live in the woods, the stumps, we are counting on you and we believe in you. She just felt tired and when she felt tired she would stress for her anxiety was at a high and she would get sick easily. When she rested for a while all this would sooner or later start to subside and she could move forth.

Please don't let us down, don't let yourself down. I know this is a great sacrifice and I know you've been through a great deal, but you have to keep going through rough times and challenges.

Augh, Amorella was frustrated and told HER, you must complete your life path for in the end you will have all that you've ever dreamed. You can do this, all you need is what you preach. Hope and faith, so don't lose it or do not push it aside. Keep going and I am at your side.

Be like no other, of what do you call yourself, human? Yes, she replied, then be like no other human and shine, Amorella said.

She told Amorella that she wouldn't give up and that she would push through the fears, the jealousy of others and the ugly envious comments of others as well, but first she needed to have a little space an meditate before the valley, Amorella agreed.

She knew that the valley would take a serious toll on her, if she did not allow her to rest. Amorella watched over her as she slept, she was tossing and turning but would at least get some sleep.

There was a secret to this valley for as you would walk through an brush up against the buds on the bushes, they would make you very sleepy. Tired even, for you could sleep hours or even days, weeks. You had to be very sharp an on guard the whole time, as to get through this valley for it held secrets. Being unaware of this, they were being watched as well but by what or whom.

As for these clover buds though, they would spray out mini pellet spears that would latch into you and cause you to sleep as they imbede in your skin. It was their self defense against swarn enemies of the cloves, these clovers were of color and beauty.

If you came across the red, blue, yellow, and green ones you'd be ok. However if you walked passed the orange ones, you would not have such luck.

Now those were the ones to watch out for an there were eight different paths to walk down, it was the matter of choosing the right one.

As they embarked through the valley, they choose the right path an made it passed. So tired from all the walking and stress, they found a spot an slept for several days not knowing some of the residue of the pellets got on their clothes and this is why.

After awaking they cleaned off their clothes, and they started up once more on HER journey, an off in the distance seen a rainbow. They forgot though that they had to see the the Magician soon before they could go forth to meet the king ... the King of Swords.

They approached this rainbow first, all of a sudden a leprechaun appears before them, his name, was Shamis. He was the keeper of the the gold an rainbow of wishes. He said, to them what do you seek?, for I know ye seek something. She spoke up an said, I'm looking for the Magician for I seek clarity and I need desperately to seek out the King of Swords.

Can you help us?, Amorella spoke up an said. For at this point she was determined to get the answers she sought out for.

He replied, you don't ask a question when asked a question. What will you do for me if I was to help you? Huh well then? Amorella replied to him, we will give you seeds for you can plant these an be able to eat on them for days at a time, it is like a full course meal. They will not go bad, but you see Shamis we must get over the rainbow. How will we accomplish this as they both stopped an looked at Shamis. He said, don't look at me that a way girls. I will help as long as, well when I need your help, you'll come right ta way.

No questions asked and that you will help me fellow leprechauns anytime they may need, even when ye be on your journey. I know it is HER, I know you have powers, that you will come into along ye way and can help us.

That could save us all from any darkness that may fall upon anyone. Being of human, myth or mystical creatures we will always need you.

Thus, will ye be the agreement between us and I will make sure the others honor our contract.

Do not betray what you agree upon for if ye do, all will come back ten fold to you, dears. Understand?, Shamis asked.

Amorella looked at HER and said, what do you think?, she said, whatever happens, what or wherever, even with whomever I will help and agree to your contract.

I have accepted that I love to help others, it's just me. I am true to my word for it is my bond.

I say what I mean, an mean what I say, for those who truly know me and see through my facoid truly know this. I will be there every step of the way with them, near or far.When it's either rough or smooth sailing, as we say back home, I will be there. If I have another whom stands by my side, as I stand by his, he to will be there when needed.

These words I promise to you, Shamis. Now ye listen close, as I tap me staff and don't fall off for thee will be made to walk the rainbow, follow the path I tell ye to go on. You must do exactly what I say, if ye don't dark things will follow you and come up all around thee, for I use the magic of the leprechauns, do ye understand this? Amorella and she agreed, as they nodded, understanding what Shamis just explained. Now, this could happen in ye spiritual realm or in ye human realm. Do as you say and stay strong with courage, confidence, and faith, remember always dear, do thus and you will remain your most powerful self.

Now, If you follow the red strip in the rainbow it will take you to my cousin Plato for he will guide you from there. He'll send you to his sister Lilith, from there she also will help ye both move forth, off you go as he waived his magic staff and pounded it on the ground.

They flew on the top of the color red part of the rainbow and followed the strip till they met up with Pluto. They walked an walked the red strip as they then seen the stars that lit up the sky, as night fell.

The blue of the rainbow got brighter an brighter, Pluto came out an shouted, WAIT he shouted, who are you? An where might you be going, whom do you seek? He asked.

They had explained to him what Shamis said, an he said, ye be gone, for I am sleepy. They said hold on where do we go?, we're to seek Lilith. She was said to be the purest of evil but in this case it was not so for they were to soon find out, these would just be more rumors from which they had heard.

Pluto then said, follow the blue strip til ye get to purple not the pink, after the blue, for you will be lost for infinity. Follow the bright white light and you will find her, she shall guide thee two to where thee need to go. Goodnight, now go, be gone, off with ya, as he stood with his little wooden staff and a smudge look on his face rubbing his weary eyes.

Then they heard a sweet, soft voice say, my dears. You both must be tired, hungry, and they replied, yes ma'am who might you be, Lilith? She said, yes dears it is I, Lilith.

Come with me an rest, eat an then I shall give you guidance on your path to the King of Swords. Your path there to him will be long. I already know this, if you are wondering for my family told me of this while you both were looking for me. Now you must rest up for you will be coming across elves, that are very sneaky and mischievous. Two of them will be no mean and rude the other on, not so much. After resting an eating, Lilith explained to them that they must be moving on to meet the Magician. Once you guys get past these little things, tests if you will.

Laughing said, then you will meet up with the Magician and then be on your way to the Kings. Your first king will be the King of Swords, an then on to the next one after that, to give you your name .

I can't believe you don't have a name like we do, I do say a prayer with that you find yourself as well as your name for Moonlight is only temporary.

Take care an best of wishes on the trails, as they fell off the white light of the rainbow and onto the pot of gold (at the end of the rainbow). Lilith to the ladies, ye be warned for whom takes from the pot without been given permission or a piece of gold hath been given to, will be of the opposite.

It'll be of cursed gold an whomever taketh it will have bad luck always, and could turn thee into something of great darkness for their souls would end up black, filth for this will be until someone could break the spell, If he or she would be so lucky. Landing on the ground not taking a piece but Lilith gave them some gold. One piece to Amorella and two pieces for Moonlight, a total of three. Towards the end of her journey, she'd find out the significance of the number three was for.

So as they walked and walked further away from the rainbow path, the started getting tired and fussing about wanting to sleep and rest and how bad they were hungry.

Amorella made up some mulberries with bread, and before she could the food appeared, it must be the luck of the gold.

Now, about thirty five miles away from the King of swords. Off in the distance was green grassy mountains with flowers and beautiful tanned brown rocks of all colors with hints of orange.

Almost after walking about fifty miles at this point, they approached the trails. Thank goodness Amorella said to her, an she said, yes, yes we made it. Finally at the trails they came across Mars. A sweet little elf whom said, ladies let me guide you through these trails.

You never know what is on these type of trails or what you might come across. I might be small he said but I'm powerful an will keep you safe .

So as they followed Mars through the first part of the trails and through the rocks an rough waters. Mars told them about a huge flower field with flowers as big as trees and there would be hidden creatures, animals an more that they had to be on their toes, for they would come across these. The girl somehow trusted Mars an walked on with him, unsure of what to expect.

Through the battle with the soldiers which they won, and fought hard to get across the trails that were full of weeds, dried grass, rocks,and dead bodies.

She made it, having never seen such a sight from where she came from, did not know what to think.

All of a sudden Uronis showed up with his shield an sword slashing through the weeds an soldiers of the Knights Clan, with Mars by his side an Amorella appeared Mercury, Mirelcka and HER as they all were given swords to fight off the Knights klan by the higher powers above. As they fought hard an proved to themselves they would win as which the did.

Slashing through giant weeds that were poisonous and had scraped Amorella. She started to fly along side her and Mirelcka slowly flying down, plummeting to the ground with a whimper.

This would be fatal with her body being so small, she didn't know what to do and turning to Mirelcka said, Amorella is injured we must save her.

Mirelcka said, the poison was working fast they had no time but to cut her and draw the poison out. However, cutting around the poison, Mirelcka was able to put her two fingers together and pull out the poison from her skin, Amorella being so tiny she wonder if it would work.

It wasn't and Mirelcka was getting nervous. Finding a tree with leaves she pulled one off wrapped it up and as she pressed her lips up against it to where the poison was. She started sucking it out for Mirelcka was immune to the poison, for it could not harm her.

She got the last of it out, and wrapped her body with another leaf she pulled from a tree. She warmed it up an placed it around her body.

Amorella would take a moment to heal, it took a few days but she'd recover fast.

The sister of Mars an Mercury, which was Mirelcka, had nursed all back to health healing each one little by little for all of them that had been injured.

All awhile this was going on, the King was preparing for HER arrival. The King of Swords and his people.

The battle was short, so bloody though and so many injured.

The knights Klan would pull out and the main knight said, we shall meet up and when we do, we will take you down.

We'll be prepared to take away your powers, for when they came near HER the knights were injured and thrown off their wild horses as they ran around and away leaving the Klan a foot, for this happening the Klan would be over powered by them all and retreated .

After the battle an them healed from being wounded, all of them needed rest and to find shelter an get their health and mind recharged.

As they sought shelter at an old torn up log cabin on the out skirts of the area which they found a little ways over the side of the mountains. Mirelcka said rest brothers an drew her sword an said I will guide them the rest of the way.

It seemed like years but only months she guided them out of the area on their horses and as they reached out of the mountain side. What was this, there were gifts all around as they grabbed all the could and all they needed, bows and arrows, food and more, scarfs for their faces, masks as well.

Mirelcka looked at HER an Amorella and said, repeat these words muliki-sham and he will appear, I must go my brothers need me, I have to finish bandaging them up.

I must be going to them for I have to help heal them. Take all the items you need and leave the other items, take what you need for you will not be able to take all of the items, the horses can not bare all the weight, you must hurry. She agreed, an thanked her for all she had done.

I must be gone now as she disappeared off in the distance, they grabbed each others hands an repeatedly said, Muliki-Sham.

Amorella, just then had a vision and in her vision she seen HER go to a bracelet she was guided to, it grew brighter with a beautiful blue glow around it. Now, as they had said those magic words a mist appeared before them, shortly after. It was the magician, they needed to have knowledge from and know how to beat off these evil attackers and creatures that they were warned about.

My lady, Moonlight and Fairy, for I will show you something's you will run into along this journey. First of all, some battles you must prepare for an overcome and next you will receive a bracelet, a ring for this will help you along the way.

Pay close attention when these pieces light up and glow. It's their way off trying to tell you something is wrong or guide you somehow to a safe place or a place you must travel.

As he said this, Amorella said, look there's something glowing blue like in my vision, behind the Magician was a bracelet that he had an as he

34

pulled around his hand, he put this on her wrist and said, take this have Faith in you, this is the Bracelet of Faith.

Now you must possess the Hope that will keep you going and the courage to keep moving forward, no matter what. Next is the Ring of Hope, keep strong.

Stay positive, for it's what drives the bracelet and ring. Trust your inner knowing and as soon as he said this he disappeared as quickly as he had arrived. Amorella said, it's time we must head to see the first king for it was the King of Swords.

The Magician would soon fade off and then it would be a ways to get to the castle. Walking for miles having blisters on her feet, tired an worn out, She was absolutely exhausted. She just wanted to leave all this and return home, the only home she ever knew before the woods and all the enchanted animals, witches, leprechauns, elves, and more.

She felt she was better off being in a home that was not so nice, then to be out here struggling to find herself, and a name.

Amorella would assure HER she would be okay an just to keep walking, reminded HER she has came so far,, to far to quit now.

No sooner, white horses either lined with gold colored saddle bags an royal blue color on them appeared, as they showed up and put their heads down, she knew they wanted Amorella and HER to jump on.

She gathered the rest of the strength she had and jumped, took the leap and as they started to ride into a beautiful kingdom they knew they would appear soon to the king, for it would be the King of Swords. They arrived to a beautiful castle an were welcomed by the commonwealth of the village, they would end up walking around. They would meet the commoners of the village, as the commoners surrounded around them. As they headed into the castle. The castle bridge around the mote came down slowly and they approached the King. He was on a horse of rarity and so big with a long white mane and brown skin, more like a bronze color and blue eyes, unlike any horse ever seen before. They would not know this was the King until he, himself guided them down the trail that lead them to the castle .

Into they main entrance way of the castle doors, as they put their horses up to eat and drink they followed him in.

The king then showed them to the main room where his thrown was and sat down, as they were surprised, they bowed before him and asked where would they go from there for they had been on a long path just to seek him.

He said, silence and listen for you must hear what you need to learn, while you are here. I must be able to train you for your up coming journeys.

As time went on and on, he taught HER patience and he taught HER his ways. She may use these skills upon her paths, so he would teach her his fighting tecniques she would fail and fail but would eventually catch on.

Laughing at her in the Spring and frowning upon her when she didn't listen in the Summer.

As it got colder, she wanted to play in the Winter throwing snow balls at him and building igloos an such, but the king, laughing deep down started to feel his cold heart warming.

She was learning, so he decided to put her to the test of all tests he had taught, would she pass?, he wondered.

Putting HER up against his best men an hardest challenges, she would prove him wrong and she passed. He was so amazed with HER.

Little did she know, he was really taken back by her, so he would put up a wall till it was time he felt he could have HER. To were he'd not fear the love he had started feeling for HER, for his heart had been cold for over ten ten long years or more.

The days has passed and they had gone, out to the garden to where she'd pass the time. Where in which she had told him she'd love to have one day, along with a garden and a bay window in a house out in the country.

She dreamed of where she could read all the books she ever wanted in the sunlight, and at night fall were she could lay and dream, falling asleep while looking at the stars. In the sky and to the moon she'd look with wonder. The King of Swords would look into HER eyes and say to HER, I would like for you to stay with me.

She said, thank you but I have to go, i must. He said NO, you will stay here and I will observe you for awhile longer before I send you forth.

Your rooms are set up now go unpack an my house hands will help you, meet me for dinner around six this evening.

Thank you kind sir, the girl an fairy said, as they followed the housekeepers to their rooms. Amorella an HER both met in the hallway of the castle as said check out my room, laughing they did as such, then she told Amorella we must get ready for dinner for it is five in the evening.

During the dinner the King would watch HER in Awwww for deep inside she took his breath away but she would never know this for he would always have a stern look upon his face an was very reserved.

After dinner an as time went on, a month went by, an then two, and then one more as the King was still in Awww over her beauty and heart but for the life of him he could not figure her out.

He knew, he had fallen for her and as the day grew where she would have to leave he explained, how he felt. She didn't doubt how he felt but deep down inside she had been so hurt an abandoned all her life till, Amorella.

She couldn't help but have doubt, for again she told him, anyone she every felt love for, left and never stood by her, for she was not a petulant child she was very independent and she knew it would take an amazing heart to mend her broken soul, so she'd wait.

It would be awhile for her to be able to grow into her own skin and realize she was okay. just by being herself, as for now well she said, I will have what I ask for, so I must keep going.

As I move forth I am seeking it out, I know deep down there is someone for me, who can teach me things and show me things I've never seen or experienced before.

He'll arrive when I least expect it and will stand his ground and stand by me, as I would him.

He'd be firm but kind, compassionate but militant, strong but wise, he will guide me and never let me go for if he will stand by my side and by me, he'd even protect me from afar.

He'd never let me down even if he could, and if we had a fight, disagreement, and separated from each other for awhile, well he'd come back, and I'd accept him back for our love will be like no others.

I know we'd have our ups and downs, flaws in all but through all that our love will prevail. As For now I must get through these battles, I know that it might be rough an seem impossible. However, I know I will conquer this and calm my demons, for it has to start with me.

She explained, she now must go like the Magician told HER, she had to have faith as she told him to have faith. What was a Summer turned to Winter, an as the snow started to fall, she headed off to the wilderness of the woods once more. The King of Swords planted her a garden and flowers outside of a bay window he had made special for HER, hoping she would again return one day, if he didn't find her first.

On the path to the King of Cups they go, however they didn't know the King of Swords was frienmies with the King of Cups and sent a letter message by his horseman as this reached the King of Cups, it read as follows:

I love her and will stop at nothing to have her with me, shall no harm come upon her I will take out your whole kingdom and anyone involved period, for now look after HER.

King of Cups laughed and when Amorella an HER arrived, he'd welcome them with open arms an his own intentions. He would prepare for a duel of the lady for there must be something about HER that the King of Swords would fall, so in love with HER.

So the King of Cups, planned to manipulate HER and giving Moonlight the finest things, showing her all she could have an more, such as gold, flowers, horses of her wildest desires, and any article of clothing. She could have her own seamstress and servant whatever she wanted would be hers.

However, this all would be a trick for he would offer to marry her after trying to kill off her friend or whomever she had with her, then eventually kill her for he only wanted her for looks, not just hers, but for his image and her magical items she possessed.

Little did he know, that had he stole them, or put them on he would turn to ash stone and die.

He was a horrid king, even though he was thought to be of love, he'd never known this, he'd only know love as material things and so he'd never be happy.

Even his kingdom was a mess and the common town folk hated him for he would only be kind to those of wealth or of beauty, if they possessed material things of fashion or style.

Amorella and HER must beware of this, they must be warned but how?, Nevertheless, this eagle would come to HER and Amorella and get HER attention by swooping down at them.

Flying back and forth over Amorella and HER heads, The eagle started screaming at HER, she thought for a brief moment and turned to Amorella an said, I wonder why the eagle showed up.

Chapter 10

What is it trying to tell us? Do we wait to figure this out or do we figure this out now? What should we do? Amorella looked at HER and said, we have to try to at least assume that something is up.

We're at the castle of the King of Cups so it must have something to do with him. Let's prepare for the worst and expect the best,okay.

Using Amorellas magic she would put up a force field around them for protection so they could sleep, for the next up coming few nights to protect them from the evil darkness that lerked around them. For it would try to come for HER and keep her away from where she was meant to go. She told Amorella that she would try, And she would practice what the King of Swords had taught her.

Through the mountain side where they would stop to enjoy the nature around them an rest up.

As the sun was setting the would see something of in the distance, as they thought it looked like another fairy but was is ?

Yes, it was Amorella friend Willis another fairy from the stump of wonders, how would he be this far away from home and why? Amorella told Moonlight about Willis and she told Amorella to go and find out, if in fact that is him. It was, Willis told Amorella,I came as fast as I could to warn you of an evil force that is brewing towards you both.

You all must be prepared this will be a battle of the most intelligent, for you must pass this battle to get to the end king.

What must we do how do we defeat them? What are these things called? Shadow hunters, Amorella said, they will steal your soul for they tend to suck the life right out of you and take your energy. I must go back now, the other fairies don't know I've gone and this is far away from home, they've warned me of the dangers that lurk.

Amorella told Willis here take this, for it will protect you going back and thank you my dear friend for I will surely tell HER an a boy we picked up along the way, Erikson. I will explain later when this journey is over. As willis flew away, Amorella headed back to where HER and Erikson to discuss what her friend Willis had told her about, and to be warned of what lays ahead. Then all of a sudden, off in the distance again they all heard something. Was it willis again? Was he in trouble? No it was something else.

Amorella said, did you hear that? What a voice she exclaimed. They waited for five minutes, Moonlight replied, I hear a fainted whisper.

It said, the King of Swords will being watching from afar, observing, you must go to the kingdom of cups and get the Ring of Luna, obtain it.

You will need this to move forward on the next few paths. The Ring of Luna, is of the moon which the ring is a spiritual ring, very important and will help us in any battles if we obtain this said ring, Amorella told her. It is said, that the Ring of Luna lays over the kingdom of cups and you must battle to even attempt to get the Ring . We must have this upon our journey .

It will glow fiery red and blue and get so big it wipes out whomever the beholder wishes, as in they will persish or it would injure them to the point they would never recover, scar them. This Ring must be obtained for if anyone is to win any battles, across these lands. All these kingdoms have the best knights and powerful warriors. So if one was to get this Ring they'd be considered, let's say powerful, Amorella said to HER. As they were preparing for battle making bows out of old twigs an wood and arrows out of metal cans, extra wood and with string the birds let lay on the ground as traps.

Now their bows an arrows were made, Amorella being so tiny, made some special arrows for her that had razor sharp points at the tip so it would pierce the skin easily.

They set off to the Kingdom of Cups, nervous about her training, told Amorella that she wanted to sit an pray at dusk for this would be a battle she believed she'd never forget.

So as dusk approaches, they kneel down an prayed to Saint Pio and Micheal for healing and for protection.

As dawn approached, their prayers had been answered. This King would put HER through the darkest of trials, she had ever been through, they would realize soon and receive their answered prayers.

She knew she had to be brave as she met him, he laughed at her for being naïve and having a sheltered childhood making fun of her saying she had daddy issues and more but what was funny to her is he didn't know her story.

She had raised herself for it was never about mommy or daddy issues is was about abandonment an stability issues and all she ever wanted or longed for was to know herself and have a name. To maybe find herself one day in life. As far as love goes she would hope for, a King to mean what he said, said what he meant, good bad or indifferent he'd never leave her side.

Guide her along her path stand his ground an claim HER love her without fear, have a strong heart for her broken soul, even if she was taking baby steps forward with growth for she'd be there for him to do the same .

So she prepared for a battle and told Amorella by sunset we will attack the King of Cups and set these commoners free.

Amorella agreed an as sun would set that very evening he made fun of her an thrashed her in front of the towns people she gathered her strength and sneaked into his room that very night, stabbing him with his own staff as she took all his riches, her an Amorella would throw out the window, to the poor.

He had always took but never gave to those whom helped him earn his riches. He treated the town folk as if they were pigs for slaughter.

They would always be indebted to her for she gave them something no one else ever has, HOPE and FAITH. She was a humble person and never knew how they felt, they would just yell out praise and thanks, with love in their voices. She knew she had to go, for killing the King was a death sentence and she would be hung if she was captured, so she hurried to get away, Amorella by her side.

The knights of the king would get close to them throwing arrows left and right. Hitting her in the arm grazing right through her shoulder, bleeding, Amorella said, we have to get you bandaged and fast.

Tying a rope with a hook from the room of the King to the wall of the castle, they would slide down. They reached the wall, as the knights shooting spears and throwing arrows at them, they made it to the bottom. Amorella said, we must get you out of here so I can try to heal you. They ran and ran, fast an far away from that horrible place. Guards hot on their tracks they moved swiftly into the night an disappeared, but not before grabbing the Ring of Luna that they had got as the king was dying. The Ring of Luna was heavily guarded in the King of Cups room, they could not believe they made it, with a smirk on her face throwing the ring into her napsack, they continued on their path. Amorella explained, we must get the arrow out before it gets infected, let's find a spot to set up for the night. As they were walking and tired an hungry the stopped to set up camp an would be visited by the Magician.

Amorella still had to find a way to heal her bleeding shoulder an take out the arrow. Amorella broke the arrow in two as she was trying to scream but Amorella put a scarf in her mouth so they wouldn't be heard.

She then took out the arrow and found some moss and warmed it, putting it on her shoulder and waiting for her to heal. Amorella again would set a invisible shield of force to protect them but what or who could break this barrier ?

The Magician, whom came an said, you must take the bracelet an go find the Golden Compass he also told them to remember what he said, Amorella thought long and hard.

He said off, by some pyramids there would be some horses and as they approached to grab the horses.

Amorella knew there was something inside the pyramids they had to obtain, a strong feeling overwhelmed her and she told Moonlight about this an so she said, then it's a must let's go we must go through all three, as I seen in a premonition of a former life.

Taking the moss off her shoulder,the wound had healed. To Amorella surprise it was as if she was never hit by the knights arrow. She was to tiny and with all the flying around she did it was hard for the knights to have her in target range, of their eyes.

Then proceeded to explain about these weird images she had seen. Writing of images which she did not know the names of but had a feeling about them.

I seen hieroglyphic images of some codes so I know how to get in them she explained. It was as if she had been there before, she had in her former past and off the went to find these pyramids.

They approached the pyramid and entered into what they would never except for their lives were at stake. That there were many dangers around them and inside the pyramids as well.

When the got in to the first pyramid, they realized it was a trap and so was the writings on the wall, to lock them in the temple for all times.

They had to figure out the codes an had a short time to do so, then the walls started closing in and they scrambled to find something to write with

Amorella found a piece of chalk an told HER to start writing, as they did the walls abruptly stopped, an they ran to the second pyramid.

This one was like the Valley of Clovers they had to find the right path or surely perish. The tunnels would be marked and they had to figure out the meanings for if they went down the one, there was a drop off onto spikes that would kill them. In another tunnel there was an illusion of steps, however it was quick sand and they'd slowly sink to their demise.

So they had to be careful and on guard. Amorella and Moonlight were scared at this point and didn't know what to do, off in the distance they had seen something.

There was a bright white gold glistening light orb that was following them around as HER and Amorella tried to shewwww it away it came closer an closer as they finally made it out of the second pyramid.

They had went through these tunnels as the shadow hunters must have followed them. They ran as fast as they could, Amorella saying a magic spell, her protection spell against them and hurried down a tunnel to the left of them.

The shadow hunters were stopped for now, as they were trying to break the barrier. They chose the right path and headed to the third pyramid.

She felt an odd feeling that they were being watched, followed. Amorella, knew that the orb was following them for awhile. They had noticed this orb since the journey into the pyramids.

They would try to shake the orb off their tail, but were not successful with that.

Had it not been for the orb of light with us she explained. We would have went down the wrong path an perished.

Maybe we should try to talk to it. Maybe not Amorella said, just keep going.

It seemed that the orb was there to help them as they moved towards the third pyramid.

Now they must figure out the last pyramid, the light guided them to a certain spot in the sand.

They were approaching and Amorella said, it's been messed with, we must dig, as they dug they found a map.

When they folded the map together it had a secret on it, it was how to outwit the third pyramid and get through, to enter.

CHAPTER 11

Amorella must remember her vision she had for it held the lock combination on the front of the entrance way to get in.

She reached her hand to turn the star shaped knob, she turned it four clicks to the left an eight to the right.

The stone door opened, and as they entered the hieroglyphs light up each step they took, through the pillars down the hallway was something glimmering.

Jumping over and through the water they found it, for it was the Golden Compass.

The light that had been following them turned into a young man, a knight for his name was Erikson and he would become HER an Amorella's good friend throughout most of their journeys ahead.

Erikson would end up playing big roles in helping HER fight off the evil forces that had followed her most of her life, especially the shadow hunters.

He would remain with HER and Amorella until the girl would find HER own light, the light she was always destined for.

With HER friends by her side, she was slowly but surely gaining confidence that she never knew she had, little did she know that Erikson was a spy, for the King of Swords.

He had his magic friend send him to watch over HER as he ruled over his kingdom and afraid she'd never speak to him it was known to Erikson he must never utter a word to HER.

He valued the king and would honor his word, to never tell her the truth but as time went on Erikson to fell for HER, he didn't look at her as a partner but as a person.

The three made a packed to always be friends even after HER journey.

Suddenly three witches came out if nowhere to battle the trio. One having dark hair, red another, and the last blonde.

The names of them they said allowed, and as follows, Trina, Teah and Tamara.

We were sent here to capture you, you killed the King of Cups an must pay.

Erikson said, for Amorella to use her protection shield and protect HER as he would go off to fight the three, taking her bow and arrows.

Erikson knew Trina, Teah and Tamara for he was a warlock spirit. He battled them, they had red glowing beams that were coming out of their hands and holding Erikson in some trance, he couldn't move and was in pain.

He resighted words of a spell and broke free. He then stood up facing the three and with blue beams coming from his eyes and fingertips he chanted his spell knocking Teah down, Tamara killing her, as she vanished. Last but not least Trina, the most powerful one of them all. Erikson would have to use all he has against this dark witch, for if they won, she would kill Moonlight and take the necklace. The necklace held special powers for it held a key, the key of the world.

It was to fit in the heart of stone that she and Amorella would later get, Erikson along their side but he had to fight off this witch.

He hurried as Trina was checking on Teah, and did an incantation spell and vanished the two, to a place called, oblivion.

He went back for Amorella an HER . They were so happy to see Erikson as they asked what happened he just said they ran from him, when he pulled out her bow and arrow.

Magician appears and tells her about her travel to the King of Wands .

Now Dear you've won the battle with the King of Cups, for even though a few had to persish an die off. Now your skin will shed an you will have anew, a beginning where you must trust the universe and your intuition on this next mission.

This will lead you South and the thing you must get, is the Golden Compass with a scale on it that represents Direction an Balance.

From that point on you will go North to you final destination. This is special and will guide you through you the paths that you take along these next few journeys towards the other Kings and there will be more trials, so be aware.

Erikson whispers to HER as says, the Compass is special it is said you can go back in time or move forward and he said we'll soon find out the power this compass holds, for I have faith you can get it.

The Balance is a thing you must possess to move forward in your journey or you will stay stagnant, you must be brave.

Being courageous- fearless ... remember there's nothing to fear but fear itself. He disappears before she could ask some questions she was confused about.

Why does this Magician always disappoint me by disappearing when I need anwsers. Amorella turned to HER an said, child be patient an still resight every word for it's like a riddle till you understand completely. What he was saying to you. Freight not for he will appear again.

Off to the temple and on their horses, Amorella an Erikson said, at the say time the King of Wands, we must go so we can get the knowledge to get this Compass. So as they headed to the King of Wands, she was nervous an knew this would be the last to the final king she'd have to encounter, before she'd get a name.

As they stop to rest, for eight days and nights, they rested and cleared their thoughts. Laying under the trees she looked up at the stars an was thinking of the final king.

She wasn't worried about the King of Wands. She was in HER head and kept having visions of the last king and what the kingdom, an king would be like.

She started to think about the King of Wands an how she would out smart him, if she was sharp enough she just needed to figure it out.

This would take her a bit to do this. She again needed to focus with no interruptions.

All she needed to do was use her intuition from deep down inside her and her telekinesis, would play a part in this as well. She would put up a wall an have all her emotions in check. She also used her telekinesis to move her sword and move other things for when battle came this would be of use, so she trained some more.

I must be at my strongest and must train mentally and emotionally for the next couple weeks or even months. Amorella and Erikson said, we'll teach you everything we know, let's do this. So outside under the stars all three held hands and prayed, asking as well to the universe and God for help an guidance and as they drifted off to sleep, unbeknown to HER the Universe and God heard HER cries, HER prayers would be answered. She would end up manifesting what she wanted an needed as well. This all would happen, time was up and now it was her turn to have everything and anything she could manifest. There would be those whom would be jealous of HER for she'd become whom she's always wanted. Be all she ever wanted, And have what she'd always dream of.

CHAPTER 12

They would try to talk trash, make up lies about her but she did not care. She'd have wealth,success, love,and her one an done.

This would happen when the rain would go away and the flowers would start to bloom, this would soon become the time this would all occur and at once. She would never go back to how she grew up and would be the first in her family, of wealth and real compassion.

This would be in the Springtime. The person or persons back home, that was so envious and jealous of HER and has wished ill will upon her and casted spells upon her, even while she was away, and horrible things that would cause her pain or grief, Karma and God would head to these people that had anything to do with this and she would feel no remorse but pray for them .

They would soon receive upon them a hundred times what they have said or done of ill will towards her, Karma and God was coming for them and would handle them, in the months of April, when it rains .

Amorella and Erikson assured her of this. Keep going forth,move. Do not let these sick people of humans through you off your path, get out of your head.

How would this be Erikson and Amorella would find out before they got to the King of Wands or at least they would hope, for Amorella told Eriksson that she believed, where Moonlight came from there were a lot of people that caused this pain for they were envious of HER because they wanted to be HER and have what she did, even though poor and having nothing.

She had confidence, love, hope, and faith. She always believed and they wanted that in themselves and as far as the boys went they were jealous always felt they could not trust her for they were the ones whom could not be trusted.

She gave her ALL to them and they took advantage of her and used her or stole off her because they were cruel or always afraid she'd leave them. Some would run away thinking she'd betray them but she was only in her head and was looking for the one to stand by her.

She felt if they cared enough, as they would tell her they did, they would have stood by her, and guided her not shamed her or put her down or left her behind.

They would have listened to her cries or her tears of joy or when she'd try to reach out to them, but they failed her. Erikson said wow, I never knew for I could never tell she's had such a hard life or trials of her own in this manner.

We must help HER as much as possible an guide her as far as she needs to go. He would be the one whom would fight for her honor, he leave all others that spoke ill will of her, as she would him for it was and would be always about respect near or far, together forever and never apart. Soon she felt he would appear.

Amorella explained, the difference between love and lust to HER, Lust is where you are in love, a wanting or believe that you are for the moment or time being.

It's a co dependent relationship and fools rush in to often, love is where the heart lies as in near or far you think of them and you carry that love with you, you'd walk away from anyone or anything that put then down. You'd fight to be better because you know you both deserve this, it's where even if a fight occurred or a disagreement happened and you both took a moment, you both would find each other and come back together.

Even stronger then before, when you reunite with you true Twin Flame or Soulmate, the feelings that you once felt will be there, for they never really left.

That is Love, True Love and your HIM is coming for you, have faith and follow your path without judgement or pain from the past but forgiveness, Amorella told HER.

Let's get her ready for these up coming tests. She will be the most prepared and the most swift an she'll come out stronger than she ever thought she could. Amorella said, she is a diamond in the rough, if only HER, HIM will come along and see this, for this would be her dream she's always wished for. Erikson replied, what the heck are we waiting for?

Let's get training HER for these tests, now let's get a move on. So it was, Amorella and the other two would soon be preparing to set up these tests for she was told she must pass, and pass all three.

However she had to pass these tests as she would prepare for at dawn.

So as the three were awaking at dawn.

Amorella said, now you must do three tests, something happened while I slept Amorella an Erikson ... what they asked I don't know I can't explain it, Moonlight replied.

It's like my strength and health, and my mental an emotional que is at an all time high. As if like my energy never left me but even though it had for so long, it's back, I'm back. She shouted with joy.

It was like months of, out of body experiences ever since I got that compass (Golden).

I would be in a room and see ones I cared for an what they were doing or saying.

I would have out of body experiences and see people I've never seen before, and things that they were going through or places.

I felt as if I once was there before. I never said anything for I thought people would think Ill of me as if I was crazy. I would experience their pain, happiness, joy, hurt and most of all love.

Amorella, I must train for this is a sign of something that I can not explain right now. I know I must do this an no matter what anyone has to say, I must go forth. Forward till I reach my destination.

She told Erikson and Amorella that this worried her and scared her at the same time.

They told her to pass these tests and soon things would be explained to her when the time is right.

Amorella and Erikson would set up three different tests for HER, each one helping her unbeknownst to her it would make her shaper, wittier faster and with that she'd take with her along to the next journey.

This making HER stronger than she ever thought she could be.

The last test would be the hardest of the all. As the first test was shooting arrows into a apple on top of Erikson head, even though him being against this, he agreed to help,for HER. Yelling at her not to miss, shaking in his boots. Amorella spoke up and said, Erikson thank you, for this would help HER with aim and skill.

This would also heighten her ability to trust her hearing for Amorella would, put something around her eyes so she had to use her senses. Next as she passed that, would be blindfolding HER and having her find her way around the trees with traps all around, this was to teach HER to trust her gut.

Her intuition, for she would have to really feel her way around. The last an Final Test would be where they took her to the caves to grab the Chalice of Fire.

CHAPTER 13

This test was a dangerous one, no one has ever completed the caves.

Was she really ready for this or would she fail? She was so nervous and her anxiety was through the roof as she started pacing back and forth debating whether or not to go in.

Taking a deep breath and a moment to think of her lessons she put on a brave face and moved ahead.

She approached the caves an went inside.

There were steps all around an spaces in between and Amorella and Erikson said, this is were you go in, an we stay here. She was scared, for if she took the wrong step she'd perish and be no more.

However, Erikson gave her a goblet from the Fountains of Youth, without spilling it she must grab this Chalice of Fire.

As she started in the cave she heard a voice it whispered in a weary scary way, make it across if you dare for you will not make it out alive.

If you don't grab the chalice for you have entered my tomb of the cave, ye shall perish as the others whom have came before thee, laughing the voice said, good luck.

She took a deep breath set the goblet down an grabbed her bow an arrow, she waited to start and the voice said again your time is running out.

You have a few minutes to get across, she threw the bow and arrows over her left shoulder and began to walk across, slipping and almost falling down to the pit of dispare.

She gained her balance an remember what the Magician said, there's nothing to fear but fear itself, now balance.

She started to the next step an step after that one, making it across to the Chalice of Fire but every time she went to grab it, the fire would rise.

It would rage out of control and screams from below would echo up, trying to though her off, she didn't budge she quickly drank the water from the Fountain of Youth and the fire dissipated, since she thought quickly and figured our the riddle of the cave. The floor grew together, all the steps merged as one. Shouting in joy, I did it. She then, walked out of the cave to Amorella and Erikson, with the Chalice of Fire.

I did it! They said we knew you would for we had no doubts.

I had faith in you all along, I have a confession though. What she said?, well I didn't set these tests up, it was really Spirit and it was only my job to guide you. All of a sudden the voice of Spirit said, you passed and must go to the third King, go and learn what you must for there is a lesson to be had.

The trio shaking off the voice but remembering what it said, they were surprised as she found something.

What was it asked Erikson? She had a surprised looked on her face as Amorella flew around her and looked as well.

She found inside the chalice was the Golden Compass, that the cave was merely a mirage, it was the third pyramid for which the compass was to be obtained, she yelled out to Spirit I was nervous, scared but decided to have faith, and to let fear no longer stop me, and I succeeded.

I will now an forever move forward for I will do my best even if I take baby steps, never back, she exclaimed with tears in her eyes. She was choked up an whispered to Spirit, thank you and thank the Magician.

Soon the King of Wands would be the next she faced, but was she ready, really ready?. Come sometime in the future, her friends knew she would have to chip away at the wall she built around her heart. So that love could come in for she would have to invite it willing, for it could not be forced But natural.

It would be like a magnetic force that would draw HIM to HER and HER to HIM, they will not get what would be happening to them or understand completely however they would just somehow know, and stay the course for all the times.

They say knowledge was always power and these two when they come together will be a force to be reckoned with. They will be the most powerful couple that many would not believe would even be together.

This couple will be of the greatest, for their love will bring them together. Marching on, before night fall and the three getting exhausted from all the things they have just overcome, Erikson exclaimed we need to get a going ladies.

Amorella said, to Moonlight, this is only the beginning. The New Moon approaches and so we must rest and eat before the Kingdom of Wands.

HER bracelet starts to light up, as the Magician appears before them, he approached and he said, to all of them the two kings have got into a battle where thousands have died, for he the king found out what happened to HER an took matters in his own hands for he valued to protect HER near or far,I must go i've said to much.

Go North now, as well you will find the King of Wands. You must again prepare for some up coming things, oh no, do you hear that?

Its chiming, they know I'm gone. I must hurry, the elders might revoke my magic for good if I keep helping you.

I must be careful whom I speak around and be careful as to how, you take this knowledge. I really must go, good luck on your path and off they all went in different directions. Erikson, Moonlight, an Amorella was headed to the Kingdom of Wands. Their travels were taking them in a weird direction, Amorella told her to pull out the Compass, as she did it pointed North, they were actually going South West.

So Erikson asked to see the Compass and guided them North.

Walking a distance ahead Erikson would ask Amorella a little more about Moonlight for she intrigued him. He would ask about her home life, where she was from and how did she get here and whom did she seek out.

He also asked what he could call her, Amorella told Eriksson that she was given a fake name by a troll to pass a bridge early on. What was it?

Erikson asked, Amorella told Erikson with a laugh, Moonlight. Her staying a ways behind and saying unto the moonlight somethings that she didn't think the other two would even remotely understand, so she sent them ahead. She cried out once more to Spirit and said, let me take these lessons and learn what I must especially from the King of Cups and Wands for that I will never let people like that disrespect me again,this I vow.

She began to turn all the darkness into light, she was transforming, with Amorella coming back to be by HER side, she would emerge into something great but what she didn't know yet. She was eager to soon find out, and what this would all mean and could she really find herself for she had been lost for so long and so much time has passed.

Now she was older an wiser, she was curious but figured she leave unto the Universe and God's gracful hands, what was meant to be will find away back to HER.

Off they trio went HER in her head once more thinking of all the pain and let downs, how people an loved ones she once invested in let her down so badly. How she never deserved such treatment as night approached they hooked up their horses and she dropped to her knees with tears in her eyes an yelled out WHY?.

Why me?, and at that very moment she looked to the sky seen a shooting star an made a wish that she'd never ever go through something like this again, love especially let alone with people. Send me a sign please let me know this will never happen again.

Then as she awoke the next morning an eagle of great beauty an strength emerged and low an behold another eagle which was rare to see, for people only seen one never two especially together for she knew deep down this was her sign.

It was a very rare experience, and she knew that someone was coming to her as she asked, she felt it.

A voice of Spirit called out, you're on the right path keep moving forward, don't look back dear and keep heading North.

She said, who are you? Why do you get in my head so? The voice said, you'll find out in time, don't lose faith, have courage and for once just be patient, trust in what you don't see allow the flow of the universe to come into you and guide you.

I shall, Spirit first I asked and you answered so I will do what you say out of respect. As she reached up on Erikson and Amorella, something was happening off center, it was a very ery weird feeling that came over her.

Right before they would reach their destination at the cottage, something happened out of the sky.

Before they reached it, rain of much force came, winds of something powerful and the sky went grey for about an hour or so. The two being nervous, she was the only one that would not be scared for drawling her sword, straight upward unto this storm In the rain. The ground was shaking, the sound of windows shattering, wood breaking, the nervousness of the trio setting in, except the boldness of Moonlight and her adrenaline.

As lightening struck all around fiercely and and moving in close, with the blink of an eye, struck her sword. Moonlights hands were shaking, she could not let go. All of her treasurers many hath given her, all lit up like the sun and she became a big ball of light, electrical currents were going in an out of her, her eyes turning from blue to white. She was glowing, Erikson and Amorella were afraid to help, so scared, they could only watch, frozen in fear.

CHAPTER 14

Moments passed and the two could only pray that she would be okay, as they watched, waiting to see what would happen next, a loud crackle came from the sky.

A blast of energy lit up not only the sky but all the land as well, it was the Universe. All powerful, colorful, energy balls entered unto her body, as she started shaking, her body fluttering falling to the ground.

In a quick moment, everything went back to the way it was before the storm. Amorella and Erikson ran to her side, are you okay? Erikson said, move as he picked her up carrying her forward away from the area. He walked an walked carrying her, Amorella trying all the magic she had to awake her, for she wouldn't wake.

Amorella, becoming more concerned she told Erikson we must stop.

Erikson came across a silver colored tree on golden grass, as he laid her down, they thought they lost her. Erickson and Amorella began to pray with tears in their eyes.

To the Universe and God almighty, righteousness, and of virtue, please help us and help out friend. She can not stop now she has to finish her destination. Please heal her for we shall be forever grateful and humble.

Erikson kept praying and Amorella had a thought and started repeating the words of Bella a witch and Venus a fairy, friends of hers.

She did this about five times, nothing Amorella tried again and her hands started moving.

Knelling down and with glee Amorella told Erickson to keep praying, its working. She continued to repeat the words of her friends, HER legs started to jerk rapidly and her eyes fluttering, she woke, weak and fragile she mustered up the strength to try to stand on her own two feet. Erikson at her side the whole time helping her to stand, asked HER are you okay? And what happened?

How do you feel? She said, I am weak but something has happened to me.I don't Know what or who or even how this has happened, I can see like I've never been able to see before.

The Universe came inside my body putting a diamond ruby heart shaped stone inside me, I can feel the energy of the Universe, as in the birds, the animals, the ground and much more .

The Universe told me, because I felt it talking to me that the more I learned to love, and to really let go of control for control is an illusion, that I'd experience things I've never felt before and have things I've never received before .

I am still weak, I need to rest Erikson, and Amorella please fly ahead and see if you can find a place for us to go. for I need to sleep and feel so hungry, it's as if I've never ate before .

Amorella replied, yes dear I am on my way and will find somewhere for us to go, she told Erikson to stay by the tree with her and that she'd be back after a bit.

Erickson agreed and said that maybe they should stay at the next place for a few weeks, even up to a month. He told Amorella that this has taken a toll on Moonlight, look at her. Clothes tattered and her eyes whitish blue, he said she is not yet herself .

Go find a place Amorella and I will do my best to care for her, till you return. I will write down everything she says and everything she does, for it could be something we need, for her as we continue forth, my friend Amorella and be safe. Amorella smiled and was gone like the wind, while Erikson was taking care of HER, she started speaking in words he did not understand, as if it was a different kind of language.

Erikson start to write down what she was saying. All he could make out was moon, sun, crescent, half, and new. She would speak of several moons an then go back to speaking in this strange language Erikson did not recognize, and was waiting for Amorella to come back and for her to try to make out what Moonlight was saying.

As Amorella was flying around, she found what looked to be a cottage. Amorella must have flown about two thousand yards before she came to this cottage as she looked through the windows and all around it seem to be unoccupied and free of danger. So Amorella headed back to tell Erikson and to check on HER. Flying as fast as she could to get them to come to the cottage she flew so fast she was wiping little nats off her face and muttering those little buggers as she flew faster and faster as she seen the tree, HER and Erikson were at.

Approaching the tree, Amorella flew down, took a deep breath for she was winded from flying so fast, her little wings and body could only take so much. She tried to talk but could not for she was out of breath.

Erikson told her to calm down an to breathe slowly, she could only get out, c c c cottage. Freeee as she took a breath. Erikson said, perfect as he woke Moonlight up for she fell asleep as they waited on Amorella.

She woke and Erikson once more by her side, he picked her up as he stood her on her feet and she said, I can walk now, just a little weak.

Erickson replied, I will hold you up and help you walk for Amorella found a cottage. Wrap your arm around my neck and walk in sync with me, as we head to the cottage, she just nodded as they set forth.

They walked and walked this long winding trail, stopping here and there to take a quick break so they could catch a moment of rest and a breath of air. She spoke up and asked Amorella how much farther my legs feel weird like wobbly and my arm is hurting from Erikson neck, Amorella said, not much further down, I can see it off in the distance.

Erikson replied, she is getting heavy, we must take one last break an then go full force ahead till we reach the cottage.

When they took this break and she was set down to rest, Erikson took Amorella to the side an told her of what she was saying while she was in this trans state, Amorella said we will find out what all this means for I know a little as far as the several moons. It is said that two moons will appear before us every four hundred and eighty years.

These are rare moons with lots of meanings we'll have to ask the Magician or someone whom knows this language or maybe she'll will come out of being so weak an know what she was saying.

Erikson agreed, and Amorella flew ahead a bit and flew back, it's around this turn and behind all those trees over there to the right side of the trail, let's go and hurry. Finally they came across the cottage for they were beat from all they had just under gone and sleeping outside wasn't cutting it anymore. As they checked out the cottage it looked empty, empty as in noone or no squatters there at all. Erikson had to do his check to be sure, even though trusting Amorella, who knew if anyone would get there before they did.

Everything checks out, he said. Amorella said, well you go in first to be sure Erikson, as Moonlight gathered up her strength, the two wasn't aware of, she would push through the two and would tell them not to be such chickens.

So as they proceed to go inside, they went into the kitchen to see if there was any food remotely around. All they found were buttons on the stove an refrigerator an remotes.

This was something they've never seen before and even asked HER do you have this back home, she said, no I've never seen such things before. She had told them she did however see these things once when she was having visions, then again when the Universe came inside her and put the Heart Stone .

She also told them that the Universe told her of elements that made up this stone and that she was chosen to carry this, from a small child they had picked HER, only when the time was right would I receive this.

I seen these gadgets in the future, later on in life. It was where I would live and spend out the rest of my years, I believe if we push on the buttons they will make items appear. Amorella said, with glee let's start pressing buttons, come on Erikson. Erikson just laughed and said okay lets.

So Erikson decided he'd push a button or two, and food already made started popping out of the oven and drinks from the refrigerator.

Wow, Amorella said, what is this place? Moonlight just walked around checking out the rooms. She could only come up with one thing, that the cottage was magic. For she went into a bedroom pushed a button on the wall an a queen sized bed appeared before her very eyes. Amorella pressed buttons in the living area an a couch and fireplace appeared, after they ate, and slept a bit, they came into the living area to sit by the fire.

They sat by the fire soaking up all the relaxing feeling that they could.

They started hearing noises, Erikson jumped up looking at all the windows and rooms and running back and forth to the living room area. He said, noone is here everything is fine. Amorella started feeling a weird odd feeling and said no, it's not over the floor started shaking and they braced themselves for what was about to happen next.

The fireplace started to change in weird funny shapes an went downwards and a man was coming up. It was the King, everyone of the trio was stunned in shock, wondering about all this magic, it was the King all along watching and waiting for them.

The King would appear before them, Amorella knowingly said, I believe he was waiting for us, because as I flew and found this place, the trees kind of parted and I could visibly see the cottage. I believe that this was the King's doing.

CHAPTER 15

I've heard about this king before, Erikson said, with a weird look on his face. When I was a ball of light, I seen four kings and I believe that the King of Wands has a little magic in him, for I seen magical things appear before me, if my memory serves me correctly. I'm not sure which king, I now know it has to be the Kings of Wands. The King of Wands, had arrived. He was a gentle king, he has a scepter and a shield with an emblem on it of a cross. Moonlight said, I apologize for I ran in here, for there was darkness falling all around an I began to let fear over take my mind for we all were extremely tired an hungry. My emotions got the best of me as well as a lack of food.

Please, forgive me and Forgive all of us. He said, come here my lady, as he put his hand on one side of her head, an scepter on the other. The King of Wands said, I release you my lady from pain, hurt, darkness, anything ugly or evil I release you. This will give you this strength from the ashes, courage from the trash, and sight from the weeds, I remove all this negative energies and bring you nothing but love, light, an positivity with prosperity. I send with you my greatest gift now be on your way for I have nothing more, be like the Phoenix and rise!

The King of Wands would pull her aside and explain the very importance of the Phoenix and the meaning of which the bird would be reborn when beaten, from ashes to fully reborn, a rebirth if you will. This would be a gift from the King of Wands, which he hath gave no other and no other would ever receive, ye after HER. The king would explain to HER of the importance of the gift she was receiving for this was a once in a life time gift. To posses the Phoenix would mean a great deal especially on the rest of her journey. She will be there when you need her most, you must posses a pure heart, of good will an intent. She will always be with you Moonlight. Go forth an seek out what you must for time is short an time is something you will never get back.

On to Spirit, she would call upon in troubled, dark times as well as happy times? Why do you come at random times and haunt me?

Tell me, I will be forever grateful, Amorella I heard spirit again for the hundredth time.

What does this mean for it refuses to tell me as I ask. Amorella said, Spirit will speak to you when the time is right and I believe each time it speaks to you, its giving you some type of clues, clues of which you need to decide what they are about and go from there.

Erikson agreed with Amorella and he told HER, remember be patient and you will find out. Somethings just take a little time, with time comes great knowledge an wisdom.

They would travel on and on, as time passed and days came, nights fell. A whisper to HER would come as the trio, Amorella HER and Erikson would lay to sleep under the moon, out in the open.

The whisper would get louder an louder waking HER, for whom is this? and why do you wake me, and not the others? If thee has something to tell me, do so now, if of good will. If not be gone and go from which you came.

The whisper said, it is I, Spirit said, time after time the answer will come when you open your heart, mind and soul. You were given the Stone of Heart, which contains the five elements of the Universe and that of life .

One is Fire, two is Earth, three is Air, forth is Water, and the fifth is the Heart, and you will find which lies within.

The Spirit spoke again and this time a little closer, louder and to the point to Moonlight, it spoke in HER ear and very clearly said, half the time you already know the answers you seek. Reassurance find that in you, you will seek what you so long for. Be still and focus for you must listen, focus an don't give up.

The full moon, anew moon was fast approaching as they laid under the brush, set up tents, and star gazed looking at the night sky.

Everyone said, goodnight and Eriksson said, don't worry for you can feel, what's approaching fear not and sleep well.

All went to sleep, she fell asleep with the moonlight gazing upon her skin as it rejuvenated HER while she was sleeping. Erikson woke to HER talking in her sleep about a sacrilegious pond, she muttered blue an white Yin an Yang, Balance. As Erikson grabbed paper to write down everything she was saying, morning was here an as they awoke Moonlight, still asleep he turned to Amorella explaining everything she had said during her sleep. Amorella said, it's a must we have to find out what this means.

Amorella told Erikson of a place, a rumor of a dragons layer. Where coy fish lay in the moonlight, a sacred place guarded by this dragon.

Chapter 16

It is said that when the one they belong to arrives they will merge as one in the moonlight, form a symbol and this sacred symbol forms as one.

The one it belongs to, they will be the balance of life for that person.

So what would all this mean, for she thought she had already got the balance she needed from the compass, which she did. It was only balance for herself, Erikson told her that he believed that this had something to do with the universe. Amorella agreed, for she told HER, the balance of of life could you only imagine. To find both, calmness inside caos, beauty within the ugly, and peace out of the storm.

There's a old wise tale about this tattoo, as she pulled up her pant leg and showed Erikson and Amorella the tattoo that was given to her as a small child. They both gasped, we must get there for it is said that this person will end up being the Empress. If in fact, it was the right person and if she could handle what would happen when the tattoo was transferred and fully completed.

This one will have the sacred mark tattooed on them, and will carry good fortune, blessings as well an the wheel of fate would change their life for the better. Erikson said, then it's a must we will wake HER an shall travel to the dragon den.

This place was a dark, dreary, dreadful place in which no one dared to venture, it was said that any that tried would burn to ashes before its fleet of knights or men that would attempt to steal the coy that lay so peacefully in the pond, as the moonlight and moon they ruled.

As they knew they had to prep for they dragons den, the had to find shelter and soon for night was approaching they found a spot closer than what they thought. They'd be next to the layer, they slept for a near three days as Amorella said, we must wake and move, let's go guys.

Erikson woke and got his gear ready, as far as HER, well she woke and got her gear on and her bow and arrows ready, she was waking rubbing her eyes and could not believe she slept so long. Amorella said, no dear you slept three days an three nights, you were mumbling things in your sleep an as she explained to HER she said I remember nothing nor have I ever heard of this but if I spoke it or of it we must go for it must be important to me on my path.

Amorella had to explain how dangerous this was an that they must kill the dragon or put him in a deep sleep for they would have to get to the sacred pond.

This would be where the coy laid and would only come out in the moonlight, for as it was told the coy,when they come together form a ying yang symbol and they form a bright light that beams up out of the den and into the sky on a circle, causing little chips of brightness which makes it look like the moon is smiling.

After all the chit chat about the coy and the rumors of them, they had to get ready for they were so close to the den, Erikson said come on enough of this we have to go, come on girls .

Once more they set forth to the dragons layer as they grabbed their things because they lost their horses back after the cottage they were on foot . A bird showed up and grew and grew into a beautiful red-orange and yellow-blue trimmed in black an white with its wings extended and a face so amazing thus must be the magical Phoenix the king of wands sent to me . It has to be said erikson, wait theres a letter attached to its ankle let's read it the girls said.

The letter read: to whom the Phoenix finds itself to, you will always have her to protect an guide you, throughout your journeys in life.

Remember; when even in hard times and things crumble into ashes, you are reborn just like the Phoenix. So, rise up again once more, an fly... signed Anonymous, can't say who I am, but you already know.

So as she proceeded, she would do her best to stay out of her head, she needed to stay focused.

After they read the letter it went up in flames, then the Phoenix started guiding them to the den, nudged HER to get on his back she said, stop you crazy thing.

Erikson and the others would laugh as she got irritated, she did her best but who was the letter really from?

She was dumbfounded as to really whom this letter could be from, while the Phoenix continued to irritate her, and everyone else continued laughing, she tried not to think about it .

The Phoenix would walk around them and try to play, this journey to the den would take close to two years, as they got close from which the came from. Had it been from where they started it would of took ten years on foot, or horse to get there.

There's a twist for the Magician said, that there would be a guy out of now where that would appear before us, and this would be like, Erikson. A guy of good faith and that she could trust this guy. How would she know and when would they find him?

The Magician had said, that he posses something that they needed to turn the tables on a up coming battle they were going to have to face. To get to the last King and that what he possesses, they will get, only if they earn his trust. For she was already told she could trust him, and that is where, faith would come in. She would have to not get in her head. Moonlight knew if that happened, it would be all bad for she would do nothing but stress an worry .

The guy would carry a crystal that she would have to obtain for it would be what activates the Heart of Stone, that was placed inside her and when this activated, amazing things would transpire, before her very eyes. She would have to stay awakened though. If she slacked she would miss the very opening she needed to find the final king. The king she has been looking for, what she thought, would be looking for answers.However, would find out it was so much more than that.

As their travels would take them to the den they would come across another guy whom was laying by the side of a Bush along the trail.

This guy introduced himself as a common guy whom was left out on the trail, by the Knights Clan, and had asked if he could travel with them. You never know I could be of some use to you guys, he said. He packed up two of his bags and Erikson said, that's fine but beware these ladies are my friends and I vowed to protect them with my life. The guy said that is fine, I'm of no harm, Amorella spoke up. Amorella asked the guy if he had a name. he said, Garaspin I am a decendent of a king, of which I know not.

I am hoping along the trail I can find some answers. Amorella said, you have to make sure it's okay with HER, she would say it was okay for someone in need, we shall help for as long as you pay it forward, I will agree to let you go with us, we shall become a team.

So as they traveled some more and got through some brush along the path, they knew they were very close and with their trusty Phoenix by their side. They knew it was about time for as Erikson and the guy they came to know over two years, Garaspin. They felt really good about beating the Dragon, Amorella would go on to get Garaspin up to date on everything they had already been through and where they were headed. She would also explain about where their final destination was, with the final king as well.

The Phoenix being so playful, it was running around like crazy and kept nudging the girl and Erikson said, awwww isn't that cute, as Garaspin would join in with poking fun. Amorella laughing as Moonlight would get aggravated, they all thought it funny. Erikson replied, he's just trying to ride you on his back. She laughed rubbed his head and said, ok you, as she jumped on the Phoenix. They embarked upon a forest of tall trees, you couldn't see five feet in front of you. The Phoenix shook the girl off reared back his head and started to glow blowing out fire and burned a path for them to cross. As the trees grew back they seen the den and as they approached, a dragon came out blaring fire for the Phoenix pushed them all aside a they began to fight.The Dragon an the Phoenix where at war,but who would win? For the Dragon it was said, that it had magical powers as well as being strong and fierce.Legend goes for the Phoenix, that it will burst into flames and battle to protect itself an those it grew fond of, and has healing powers from the tears it cries. It was hard for a Phoenix to tear up. Going forward it was time, for the battle is beginning.

The battle begun as the dragon would fire flames at the Phoenix, the Phoenix would turn to ashes an reappear on the other side of the dragon, then the other side scorching it all over, an this happened over an over, needless to say the Dragon looked to be getting the better of the Phoenix but once more he arose to bury the Dragon in ashes and as the Phoenix walked over to HER, Amorella and EErikson. Moonlight screamed out, help me please because the Phoenix wasn't returning from the ashes. as the battle was continuing Erikson and Garaspin so brave, grabbed a vial an went to the Phoenix, as the Phoenix teared up and grabbed the Phoenixs tears, it is said has healing powers.

Pulling out the vial an sprinkling a tear or two over the Phoenix.

Waiting patiently for the Phoenix to heal. They would all pace in nervousness for the Phoenix was not just a bird of myth, but was their friend.

As they kept watching for awhile one moment to the next, then he arose and reemerged as they started in the den after she hugged the Phoenix and he nudged her. She knew he'd be okay, for he was weak but she'd be back to her fun, loving, and aggravating self, soon.

They all knew the Phoenix would guide them. So they all looked to the Phoenix as They walked in the layer she had a vision, of all her ancestors before her, she was staring down at a running river of water in the den and just stopped.

They said to her, it is time for you to emerge and obtain your powers, so go forth and find your answers.

They walked down these creepy watery halls, with glistening crystals all around it yet was so amazing and stunning. So she knew she needed to explain somethings to the team before they presumed any further, Because she had another vision and while this would happen she had headaches, short lasting, still her head would hurt an she would have to pause.

She continued to explain what she had seen though her vision. They all carried on the path in the caves as the Phoenix was guiding them. As she came to she explained, to the group the rest of the experience, as they set forth trying to figure it out.

She came across the Sacred Pond of the Coy and as moonlight was fast approaching out of nowhere there was one coy beautiful blue an then another a beautiful pearl white as they came closer together they merged into one. When they merged, it reveled a tattoo Yin an Yang, her leg started to light up it was HER, that the coy belonged too as her tattoo was glowing, it was Moonlight.

In every moonlight, they would be with HER no matter where, when, or what case it might be. As the moonlight started to dissipate, the coy broke apart going to each side of the pond, branding HER as theirs, an HER merging with them as they were hers. She knew she was on the right path of her journey and set forth for it almost time for the very last King. She would be more confident, as things became more surreal.

Garaspin spoke up, I don't know which way to go the walls are starting to crumble down. Erikson the path caved in, said Amorella. Moonlight and the Phoenix headed to the next path of the caves to find a way out.

They had to move, for the den started to come down all around them and she wanted to grab the coy an Amorella spoke up, they are fine an underground. We can always come back an dig up the rubble, for now we must go, Now running from the crumbling den, they were about to come across a town and little did they know to their surprise they had another battle to surcome for this would be the battle of the 33rd.

This would be the town, that the battle would take place at, by the ruins.

Garaspin said, it has been a pleasure and for you saving me, I will stay behind and guard the coy, after I dig up all the rubble and debris.

Don't worry, I will make them safe and I shall rebuild here, where I know I am safe. For once I will get all this done, I will find my way back to my family from which I came and the king which I am a part of.

She hugged Garaspin and kissed him softly on the cheek and Amorella said, her good byes as well. Erikson punched him in the arm and then hugged him and he said, take care man I hope you find your family, I believe for your sacrifice for HER and helping the coy, it will happen for you man, stay strong.

Garaspin said, thank you all, best of wishes on your path, be safe and guard each other well. As the Phoenix ran up to say its goodbyes knocking him down and licking his face, she spoke and said, come on let's go for we don't have much time, hopefully we cross paths again Garaspin. I bid farewell.

As they started back on their path she felt safe as in Garaspin taking care of the coy and helping them all rebuild. So at that point she had no worries but as for what was coming, she had no idea, they however hadn't any clue. Right before the next up coming trial, they would encounter a witch.

A Witch for whom was blind, running from the dragons den an old man grabbed HER hand as they bumped into each other, he felt HER energy. He knew she was of love and light, that she had a pure heart.

He stared into her soul with his mind, that she'd be the one the ultimate KING would take for all time and give HER unconditional love and protection, and to stand by her when all else crumbles, he would be the one to give HER a NAME. The old man could not tell her this but told HER, you have someone coming for you with a great deal of abundance for only you child.

You have only a short time before he arrives oh dear, oh dear, I've said to much. She kissed the blind old man on the cheek and said, it's ok and I'll be fine for I am on a journey to seek out the King of Pentacles, for he holds a clue to what I seek on my path. The old man replied, you have not long dear before he arrives, you must prepare yourself for him for he is a strong, stern, wise King for he holds a lot of clout so keep in mind for he is kind. Tells no tails for he holds the key of information you need, for you'll be given a name and glow, with that you must go. I bid a dew and wish you many blessings, set forth don't fear the Lord and head out towards, HIM.

Out of nowhere he vanished, as they looked around for the witch they would not be able to find him. They all turned an looked at each other shrugging their shoulders and with that the witch disappeared.

They had to hurry and set out to find a place to camp for a few weeks for they knew they were the closest, that anyone had ever been from Moonlights land and way of life .

Up there, outside the woods where everything people thought was reality, how they were taught was not really the case. It was actually, whatever they learned growing up, for that became their reality.

So you see things are never as they seem and reality is what you make it.

As you see, they all wore rose colored glasses and as far as HER, well she sees all now, she is awakened and will move forth with class and grace from this day forth, Erikson said.

So as they had rested and ate, geared up along side the Phoenix, she knew it was go time she was trusting her intuition this time and knew a battle was fast approaching, she soon had a headache and was remembering something Garaspin had said, about being dumped on the side of the trail by the knights Klan.

She wondered, if maybe, just maybe the feeling she was getting would in fact be a battle with them to get to the king she needed to see, finally.

As they rested in an area that was of statues an tombs, walls of stone that were torn down it was the Ruins of The Ravens .

The reason for this name was etched in the stone, for it said that the ravens would one day come to this place to live and stay as guardians for the ruins.

As the sat around talking about their next moves, they were being watched but by who, it was the huntsmen of the town .

HER feeling was surreal and her intuition grew deeper for she knew they would have to prepare and gather up anything that they could for battle.

They knew the had to rest so as they watched, the huntsmen went back to report but they failed to report the Phoenix for they didn't see him, he was off gathering food for the trio.

So, they did not report this to the king there. The Phoenix would be gone for atleast two days away from the team as it was grabbing food for them, enough for them to eat for a week or two.

The Phoenix would come back to the camp and realize the group was gone, not before the girl left the Phoenix a sign that they were captured, she had left the Phoenix her favorite scarf and in it was her bracelet, that was so important to her.

The Phoenix took brief action to access what was going on and with fast action took flight to go to the town, in which its friends were being held captive.

All of them being in a cold, damp dark place were trying to put a plan into action for they would take a stick found on the dirt ground an Erickson would try to draw a plan of action for the battle, they all would input on these plans of action as they all brainstormed. Waiting for the moment they were taken to the battlefield.

Now, was the great duel in the town of nowhere. So as night fell the trio was resting and Erikson was abruptly woken by hoof stomps an horses, he had thought he was dreaming but it was the Knights Clan .

The Knights Clan captured the trio, Erikson, Amorella and HER,

They were taken to the dungeon where they would sit for five long days, as a knight said to them in the dungeon he said, you battle at dawn for no one embarks on our land uninvited. They tried to explain about their journey to the King of Pentacles, the knight replied, silence. We don't care about your excuses and with an evil cackle, the knight left.

They knew without the Phoenix they were in trouble, they needed to come up with something and fast. Amorella said, can you call to the Phoenix somehow? She explained, she left the bracelet wrapped in her favorite scarf for which the Phoenix would know that they were in trouble and could follow her scent.

The three had to come up with a plan, Erikson said, we can use the Ring of Luna and the bracelet, right?

No silly, I just told Amorella I left it behind so the Phoenix could find us, and help get up out of here before the duel.

Amorella trying to stay positive said, wehave to have faith, at that moment on HER the Yin an Yang tattoo started glowing, kowing she had the power of the moonlight and sacred coy fish. She felt somewhat relieved as dawn approached, the knights approached and came to get the three from the dungeon, heading towards the ring the trio started to plot a escape from that town. Just then Erikson was thrown into the ring. As everyone in the town showed.

All three of them, Erikson, Amorella and HER looked around at the towns people, they were laughing at them an throwing rotten food at them, one said, don't waste the food on the filth. Amorella said, to HER just ignore them and keep your head held high, right Erikson?.

Erikson was more worried about being in the duel than anything but agreed with Amorella.

Without a moment's notice, the crowd starred going crazy wild.

The blacksmith from down the lane that hated being there would soon hear of this and make something for the trio, especially Erikson.

His name was Heath, Heath was a very talented blacksmith made a special sword lined with crystals to make the blade sharp and swift, so he made the blade thin an dull.

While heath was fast at making, he knew he had to get it somehow to them, as he was searching outside of town for these crystals he ran into the Phoenix and so they made friends and quickly he hid the bird as he came into town an to his shop.

He had help with the Phoenix as the bird would heat up the metal so he could make the sword, as it was almost completely done. Heath was planning on getting the sword to Erikson. However, knew he would need a shield an if he made for him it would be admissible in the duel, or you had to make your own.

Erikson was thrown a wood staff and very little armor and a white horse that would barely budge on the opponent's side at the other end of the ring, was a knight in full body armor and a steel staff on a black horse that at any moment was ready to charge on command, no sooner a moment passed the ring leader yelled out, charge as Amorella an HER watched in fear.

CHAPTER 17

The knight came up upon Erikson knocking him almost of his horse, stabbing him in the upper right shoulder, bleeding but not bad Erikson regained his stance an moved up upon his horse, again without warning the knight struck Erikson again this time in his left upper shoulder trying to make it where he couldn't even hold a staff.

Erikson bleeding bad at this point from both his shoulders,Her and Amorella ran to his side using the magic of the Ring of Luna and the bracelet told him with a whisper, you got this ...

get him when he looks to the right of the crowd, in his abdomen stab him then go for his helmet for there's a weak spot in it, for it wasn't put together well and that's where you will have him.

You have to take him out, no questions asked this must be done.

As they told Erikson you must win this or we will be slaves forever in this town an you will persish now go and fight with all you heart for now you possess the knowledge of what you must do.

Right then heath showed up with the Phoenix, and had the Phoenix fly him the sword and shield for which he would use to finish the battle.

Erikson got back up on his horse after HER an Amorella cleaned him up and at full force charged at the knight stabbing him in the abdomen and then went for his helmet, cracking into two no three pieces Falling off the Knights head which was considered a disgrace as it was an automatic loss for the knight the crowd yelled out finish him.

Erikson shoulder was killing him but he mustered up the strength from the Ring of Luna and swinging his staff around and around with a whooshing sound, he stabbed the knight in the arm and then in the leg, as the crowd kept chanting, finish him!

Erikson could not for he showed the knight mercy then turned to the crowd an said, maybe ye all should learn mercy for then maybe your town will thrive for I will not kill. Just then HER tattoo of the coy started glowing again and out of no where the Phoenix appeared and grabbed up the trio and flew them about five hundred miles away so Erikson could eat, rest an heal. Amorella got into Eriksons napsack then she grabbed the vial of Phoenix tears and poured it over his wounds.

Forever grateful for Heath, as Erikson would leave to her the sword an shield of crystals as he called them. Please, Express my greatest gratitude to Health for he helped save us all, she said, I will, this I promise to you, Erikson.

Instantly Erikson began to heal but was so exhausted he passed out from all the pain and just slept. It seemed like several days an nights, Amorella knew they were getting closer an closer to the King of Pentacles and away from dark times. Right out of the blue the Phoenix looked at HER an rubbed his head up against hers and started to tear up and let out a cry. She caught fire an turned to flames just before that taking Erikson with her, a note from Erikson was left.

It read my fair lady, I was only an illusion of your mind, one the King of Swords sent me out of love for you. Healing, I must go for I did my do diligence and protected you from harms way. Take care my friends for you will always be in my heart, she yelled and cried out, Erikson you were my close friend an for your loyal an teachings I will never forget thee. Please can I do anything? Please don't leave me, she cried out .

It was of no use, Erikson and the Phoenix were gone, but will never be forgotten. Amorella and the girl made a statue of them both, were last they lay for they will always be remembered.

Amorella knew that the girl had to pull herself together once more for the final journey was so very near, she told HER to get ready night was upon them.

As night approached Amorella knew their luck would again change for the New Moon was coming up upon them, it was the moon of blessings and luck, The MOON of GEMINI.

This is said many moons ago that the moon of GEMINI only comes once every thousand years and that the one that holds the Heart of Stone and has the special tattoo . Which she will end up being able to use all the gifts God and the Universe has gave her from birth, for this she'll be granted.

This said, this was and is her birth right, she will be the Empress and end up with her final Emperor. The moon with shine so bright and a beam will come to HER as she sleeps and kiss her with special powers.

For all times, she will wake and know for she'd have all the knowledge in the world.

It was time to meet the King of Pentacles for he embraced HER an Amorella, took them under his wing as if the belonged at the castle with him, instantly she knew he wasn't for her or her greater good an this would do nothing if she was to stay.

So her an Amorella planned to leave in the middle of the night, like thieves in the wind, even though he was great to her an Amorella, fed them and clothed them.

Anything they needed was theirs or even HER wants the king provided for she knew it was just a matter of time for she was so used to being independent and a survivor, she would not or did not know how to act, but knew she would have to leave, for she did not want to break his heart.

Only thing she could offer was love and loyalty. The King of Pentacles had done so many nice things for her, as she was reminiscing and looking at the two long years there, for this king made her a baby window of the Southwest end of the castle along with a bookcase as big as the sky, all he wanted was to love her always.

She remembered he begged her not to go, for she was sad she knew she had to finish HER journey for she never knew stability or what it was to be stable.

She always thought it was the other person and when she'd realized it was her, an how she had control issues, for to truly love she'd have to give up these toxic traits for a healthy unconditional loving relationship.

She was waiting for the one that would always stand by her, no matter what and so with that she knew what she had to do for herself.

She was determined to drop these traits and thanked the king for guidance and helping her to really open her eyes, for she'll no longer be blinded by the darkness, that had fallen upon her for years.

Amorella heard HER cry out in the night " tell me " she heard nothing ... She yelled out I've always been abandoned and never knew stability, when I get ones I care about they are taken away whyyyyy?

She had all these gifts and didn't know how to use them for no one has ever taught her.

It seemed as if she'd never have what she's always wanted, she knew she had to stop thinking like that for it was never what she wanted but it was always what she needed. That she sought out for and when she figured this out, she'd be free of all the toxicity that plagued HER life and so forth an so on, Amorella told HER before to remember what her lessons were.

CHAPTER 18

What she was taught by them, she needed to remember, she told her before that this will help her along her path of journeys.

She would scream out once more to Spirit, I have been tested and had many failures Also many successes. I have passed some tests and have failed some, I need answered, now.

Please, as tears streamed down her face for what Moonlight would swear it'd be the last time she'd ever shed a tear for herself let alone I am ready! anyone.

Show me love …

I am not scared.

I know an have learned self love.

I am not scareddddd.

I know now what I want, for I am ready again, once more to give my all and do it right by loving myself along with what my needs and wants are I can do this …

Answer meeee she cried out, for I am tired, the voice of Spirit came an said " not much longer for he is looking for you".

Amorella was so confused, and Moonlight (HER) asked who is?

What are you talking about?

Spirit replied, he's coming back for you, anew, a rebirth, be on your way before it's to late and find your light …

You must go now the last one is waiting upon your arrival, for through the darkness day in, an day out.

She would find her way, there is one last test for you must pass, it's the test of Truth and Trust. Can you manage this my dear for this is the final final test before HE arrives.

After this test, you will know your worth. The something you have yearned for all along an you did not even know it.

Amorella said, to Her let's do this, we've beat every test before. I surely know we can bet the Truth an Trust test, lets go.

We went forth into the early evening and found a stone table, on that table laid a black an white cougar, the cougar of truth an knowledge, as they approached the cougar woke and yawned an said, who embarks upon my truth an the trust of stones for this place is forbidden.

She told cougar she had found a map, deep in the sand that uncovered many secret places and when they folded it, this spot appeared on the map and spirit said to set forth, for it was part of my journey. We apologize for waking you, while you were in deep slumber.

Cougar roared and said, you seek out HIM, unconditional and reciprocity in love, am I right? She got very quite as it was like the cougar read her mind as the cougar circled around Amorella and HER, she got nervous but remembered to trust, and so she did. The cougar asked once more am I right?. Hoping she'd lie an he could eat her, she answered and said, yes you are correct cougar now what must I do or use on my next path to travel to HIM.

I must find him for I know he's been looking for me, I can feel his energy, it has been with me on and off this whole journey. Cougar said, take the Truth an Trust and you will find him now go before I eat you.

You don't have much time as my hunger is getting the best of me and I cannot control the animal inside me that rages.

She said, I thought if I did what you asked you wouldn't harm us. He said, I did not promise that I've not ate in Years as well …

I'm getting hungrier by the moment, with a loud roar he said GO an don't look back, for if you do you, the test will start all over again.

Trust … you will find your Truth soon.

Running from the cougars table, they did not look back an was exhausted, she had to get her energy up she must eat an rest at this point her sleep came first, they would look for food at dawn.

She did not want to get sick again and just stay stagnant, it was time she was in a routine even through all of the rest of her journey, soon she'd be at the point of her destination and never look back.

They found food they ate and rest they did, the eagle soared out of the sky, and guided them throughout the night time. Calling out for she knew what was about to approach them For the shadow hunters, came out of no where, screeching a horrid yell.

Trying to get to Moonlight, Amorella and the eagle took action fast to blow them into bites and pieces, combining magical powers.

She laid to the ground till Amorella told her it was safe to stand again.

With the shadow hunters gone the eagle saved them from the darkness an then flew away.

They started towards a glistening lake off the South end then North of the lake, direction as where the compass had taken them too.

She rubbed her eyes as she seen another shadowy figure, Amorella, do you see what I do? Amorella replied, yes I do.

As they got towards a shimmering shadow, she was nervous but no longer scared. By the lake, there was something that felt familiar.

So as she walked confidently and proudly to the water, that was flowing slowly and glistening, butterflies flying all around.

She heard the trees call to her as their leaves swayed back an forth, they said, "This is it, he is here, your King, for it is HIM.

Do not be scared of him, he will not allow that., he will never let you go, go forth.

It was the one she waited for, longed for, all her trials and tribulations, things she'd never seen before or been through. Amorella said, go to HIM.

He has been looking for you, as you waited and looked for him. Go forth and claim what is truly meant for you.

No, what's this he's walking to you, out of this mist that appeared before them. It was the King of Pentacles, so as he took HER hand, He said I am loyal, dependable, faithful.

She told HIM I am scard up, broken if you will from all my battles I have faced and loves I have lost.

He said, let me guide you, let me be there for you, let me love you. I will heal your soul as I have a big heart an would like to share this with you, I will make a promise to never leave your side.

As she was thinking, she knew how she felt about HIM, he stepped a few steps back and all of a sudden, three kings before him showed up out of the mist.

The King of Cups, the King of Wands, King of Pentacles, and the King of Swords (the one she was most fond of would be them ALL), they started to merge together as one to form the Emperor and Amorella could barely speak at that moment, the fairy started to merge with HER as she was staring up at the stars.

Light glowing all around HIM and light shinning beams out of HER, it would be something of the most amazing things that would happen of all time.

She was getting her wings as they started to reemerge from her back and come to find Amorella was really the angel inside her, for the final king broke whatever curse she had ever had, HER wings beautiful an bright for she would start soon to merge into whom she was always meant to be.

It was then she found the angel inside her, as they looked at one another, He looked to HER an said, our journey was written but never was our destination. He as well got on his knees asking for her forgiveness and told HER:

I will be anything for you, please forgive me for taking so long. I will lay my life on the line. I get it now. We are from two different worlds, now I will with your permission at my side merge them together, forever.

I will cross the ocean for you, I will go and bring you the moon. I will be your strength when you are weak, anything you need. I will be the sun in your sky.

I will build a strong tall fortress to protect you. I will fight for you, with every breath I breathe, with my soul I will give you the world. All you have to to do is put your faith in me.For, it was the angel inside you, all along that brought you to me, for I knew you were waiting for me an I was looking for you, and now we found each other.It's our time to be away from all this drama and focus on us, free from others. No one will again intrude or interrupt what we share.

He took the rains by storm and she knew he would always be there, never to leave nor would she again leave him. Trust an faith was now and forever in them for they shared a bond that nothing could break., she agreed.

I now give you a name, she replied what name, he said my name for it'll be yours for all eternity as long as you will keep it .

She replied, I shall for always for you are my HIM and with that he replied, an you are my HER …

With that they started in the direction of the lake and disappeared into the night mist.

What will your future hold?

Well … It is your journey so find your destination.

The rest is up to you, for you to decide.

By: R.A.Bullis

This Book is dedicated to,

GOD

My one and done (W. BROYLES),

R. KATZ,

MY MOTHER(ALICIA HASTY),

MY CHILDREN (KATELYNN MULLINS, JALEN GREGORY AND DESTINY BULLIS).

TO ALL THOSE WHOM EVER FELT HURT, PAIN, HEARTBREAK, LOVE, OR BEING LOST HEARS TO YOU....

DON'T GIVE UP AND DONT GIVE IN FOR THERE IS A RAINBOW THROUGH THE STORM.

TO ALL THAT BELIEVED IN ME!

Printed in the United States
by Baker & Taylor Publisher Services